To Samir,

Glad you could make it!

I hope you enjoy the story.

Shepherds of Sparrows

An Okal Rel Universe Legacy Novella

By Hal J. Friesen

Hal Friesen

realityskimming**press**

AN IMPRINT OF OKAL REL UNIVERSE

BURNABY, BC

Reality Skimming Press
An Imprint of Okal Rel Universe
201-9329 University Crescent, Burnaby, BC, V5A 4Y4, Canada

Interior design: Janice Blaine
Cover art: Maja LaValley
ISBN: 978-0-9921402-0-5

FIRST EDITION
(C-20131024)
okalrel.org

Dedication

For Grandma, my creative shepherd.

Chapter 1

Shoulders squeezed Olivia from all sides as the crowd roared in anger. Her father walked out onto the Challenge Floor of Grianach District on Monitum, which was nothing compared to Fountain Court and seldom used. Today, however, the public had taken exceptional interest in the court's dealings. The cramped amphitheater held more than two hundred people—well over the maximum number of occupants. It seemed as though everyone who knew about the atrocity had shown up.

Although her father's face looked calm, Olivia could see the veins protruded prominently on his sword hand, a sign of his trademark fist-clenching as a way of coping with stress. Olivia could remember his hands when he was trying to explain that grandpa had died. The way he stared and clutched them as though they might hold back the tears. Or the time when he had gone off to help in the Nesak war, and had waved goodbye with fake promises that everything would be all right.

"Ow!" cried Voltan, her younger brother, pulling his hand away from hers. She looked down apologetically and rested her hand upon his head. His smooth, childish face was creased by a deep frown and a furrowed brow, a common expression for him, but Olivia imagined it was worsened by his worry for their father. For the first time in her life, she found herself wishing that the law could be carried out with a means other than swords.

Cana Grianach, the challenger, walked onto the floor, and cheers of encouragement rang out. He had a predatory smile on his face, looking around at the crowd with his arms raised as though to imply, *I've got the world on my side.*

Olivia scanned the few places where no one was cheering, and caught sight of her mother a third of the ring away from her. Although she had trimmed her hair and put on a bit of make-up, Olivia could recognize her. She was searching, scanning for them, and Olivia shrank a little. She and Voltan had come here against their mother's wishes, knowing that it might be the last time they would see their father alive. Her mother feared she wouldn't be able to protect them from the mob, but Olivia felt that the Monatese were better than succumbing to mob mentality, even in a case like this one.

We didn't need a better life, Daddy, she thought sadly. *We had a great one.* She wondered what exactly was coursing through her veins that was so wrong. Supposedly her father's transgression had made her a highborn instead of a nobleborn like almost everyone else on Monitum. Being highborn would grant her privileges no regular Monatese citizen would ever have access to. As a highborn, there was even the possibility that Olivia could hold a position of power on Gelion, the center of the Empire where the divided Hearths jousted for power on the octagon known as Fountain Court. It was a world she'd thought was completely out of reach, and it still seemed intangible as she stood beside her brother among the masses.

She didn't feel like she belonged to a higher class— in fact, with how angry everyone was, she felt lower. They considered her father's defilement of his body to be *okal'a'ni* in the worst way imaginable, tainting not only his soul but the bodies and souls of all future generations descended from him. At least, that's what most argued. Her father's manipulation of body and soul was why he might die today.

A blinding light flashed in Olivia's eyes and her knees buckled. She felt a clear dream coming into vision, and snapped her attention back to reality, back to the feeling of her brother against her and the need to protect him. Gasping for breath, she opened her eyes to the sight of Voltan's wrinkled shirt as he hugged her, enthusiastically smiling at anyone who glanced their way. *He's playing the bloodthirsty part well,* she thought as her mind regained its balance from the torrent of emotion.

"I can't wait for the fight," she lied, smiling with the fakest smile she could pull off. She bent and whispered into Voltan's ear, "Thank you."

The shadow of a sour expression crossed Voltan's face again, but he put back on the façade of enthusiasm just as quickly as Olivia had noticed it. The judge of honor had begun reading the charges, a skinny man who, to Olivia, seemed too inexperienced to be casting judgment.

"Laedan Ald'erda, vassal of liege Monitum, you are hereby charged with the crime of committing *okal'a'ni* sacrilege of your own body, and passing that onto your off-spring. The Watching Dead weep with anger at your betrayal of your family and of all of Sevildom. The charges were laid by Cana Grianach, and the challenge is to the death."

Olivia's vision blurred again, but she fought back the tears and emotion, trying to focus on the memories of when her siblings had needed her most— when her mother had been a wreck after Laedan's late return from the Nesak war, when Voltan had been cruelly beaten by the hospital kids and she had acted as resident bully to protect him.

The fingers of her free hand ran along the surface of the curved sphere she wore about her neck. It was supposed to be carved into the continents of Old Earth, although Olivia had no way of telling if that was true. In the indents of the oceans were carved tiny, almost unreadable prayers for love and continuity. Olivia's father had brought it back for her from the Nesak war, as though it would serve as a good luck charm against planet-destroying conflict. Conflict he'd hoped to leave behind in the cold reaches when he returned home.

Laedan, Olivia's father, merely nodded at the charges laid against him, sweat now visible on his brow, his mouth a straight line. As the judge of honor initiated the fight, Olivia caught the sudden movement of her mother far away.

Mother had run through the crowd to snatch at Olivia's older brother, Pleo, who had gone missing even before she and Voltan had snuck out. Pleo looked afraid and ashamed, pushing away from their mother with nowhere to go. Her pursuit continued as the fight began and the two men circled each other on the Challenge Floor. The crowd threw jeers and shouts for Laedan to get dunked, which from the little Olivia knew of *rel*-skimming, wasn't possible in a swordfight. *Pleo, where have you been?* she thought, wishing she could protect all of them.

Her mother caught Pleo just as Cana slashed Laedan's upper arm, eliciting a raucous cheer from the crowd. Voltan flinched beside her, and she moved behind him, putting both of her hands on his shoulders a foot below hers. "He'll make it," she whispered.

Voltan said nothing, and Olivia wished again that the overexcited, overly talkative Pleo were with them, if only to distract her from every dive, dodge and parry that threatened to make her heart explode or her consciousness dip fully into a clear dream. An episode wouldn't end well, since people had already begun to make the connection between her clear dreaming and her father's manipulation of genetics. She doubted she'd be able to explain it away as a Golden Demish trait inherited from her long-lost grandmother. She swallowed, her throat dry.

The fight was quick— nothing like Olivia had read about in the local branch library of Sanctuary. After a clash of metal and a flurry of movement, her father stepped backward with a bloodied sword. Cana fell to the ground, a red pool forming on the smooth tiles.

For a moment, the crowd hushed, as though they had all just exhaled and forgotten what came next. Olivia's mother's cry of jubilation broke the silence, and everyone in the amphitheater immediately identified her despite her makeup and new clothes. Movement stirred as murmurs went out, and Olivia felt her skin turn cold. She saw a horrified look on her father's face that must have mirrored her own— she had inherited his keen sense of atmosphere.

Run, Mom, she thought, and opened her mouth to shout it. The only thing that stopped her was the warmth of Voltan against her, who had taken his turn to squeeze her hand so hard it would be bruised tomorrow. They might all die if Olivia reminded the crowd of her and Voltan's existence. *What have I done?* she thought, her heartbeats quickening. Her mother might not be here if it hadn't been for Olivia's desertion.

The murmurs turned into shouts of anger as the crowd started to descend upon the Challenge Floor. The blood drained from Laedan's face as he froze and stared at the encroaching mob. A second later he sheathed his sword, and said two words that were lost in the cacophony.

"*Ack... rel,*" Olivia said in a gasp, as her vision turned white and she fell to her knees. The visions of a clear dream took her, a ringing blast that was indecipherable from the mob's frenzy.

Chapter 2

"I'm only staying if my family can as well," said Nestor, standing with his feet wide in Di Mon's large study. The walls were adorned with green Monatese drapes and imagery of Earth. Di Mon, liege of Monitum, paced back and forth in front of him, his face crumpled.

"You don't want them to be here," said Di Mon angrily. "You have no idea what's going on yet. And your family can't know, even if I tell you."

Nestor stared at the stubborn man in front of him, the liege who seemed ready to slash him down any second. He had known Di Mon for a long time— fought beside him, and penetrated his darkest secrets, unbeknownst to Liege Monitum himself.

Nestor knew Di Mon wouldn't hesitate to strike him down if he decided it was necessary, but Nestor was arguing a point he could not negotiate on. Not since his son had been kidnapped by the notorious gangster known as the Caddy. "Then you can get someone else to help you," Nestor said.

Di Mon stopped moving and vibrated for few seconds before replying. "You can't take them with you to every reach in the galaxy!" he shouted.

Whatever was going on in Grianach District had the usually controlled, if high strung, liege of Monitum wound up to an unusual pitch of temper.

An errant burst into the room and Di Mon brandished his sword. The errant, inches away from the tip of the blade, trembled as he stuttered. "M— my liege, the duel's going forward. Immediately."

"What!" Di Mon snapped, in a white rage.

"Th— the local authorities said they h-hadn't received your request to convene a preliminary inquiry to—"

Di Mon cut him off with a gesture. He sheathed his sword and grabbed Nestor by the shoulder in one fluid movement. "Fine," he said to Nestor, "but you will be responsible for ensuring your family's discretion. Their complete ignorance would be best! This is an ugly, explosive business, Nestor. The kind of thing the rest of Sevildom will lynch the Monatese for if we show any hint of tolerance. In fact, I don't want to find out how they'll respond. I want all knowledge of it dying out in Grianach, where it started." His eyes focused on something far away and began to scan as though Di Mon had to dig deep for answers— something the liege almost never had to do. "I don't think Laedan's the only one…"

Nestor's skin crawled as Di Mon continued, as much to himself as to Nestor.

"Grianach is an isolated district, for Monitum, except for the spaceport. Limited in its connections with more cosmopolitan centers. It might be possible to cauterize it here. And as far as reducing the harm to the innocents involved, if there are any— if it gets out, we'll have to be even bloodier in our demonstration of retribution in the clean-up. Is that clear?"

"Clear," Nestor assured his friend, although he found the lack of detail unnerving. He was just beginning to guess why Di Mon needed someone unconventional to be his agent in the Grianach affair, someone he might also trust to be his conscience— unofficially. And that was both dangerous and disturbing.

They left the local Green House — House Monitum's local outpost of government operations — in an awaiting car and were stopped far from the grounds of the Grianach amphitheater by hordes of people blocking the road. Nestor was shocked when no one in the crowd made any attempt to move at the sight of an official vehicle. Di Mon cursed and jumped out. He and Nestor unsheathed their swords and their approach finally cleared a path into the amphitheater. The hairs on Nestor's back prickled as he felt angry eyes staring at them. Di Mon had not given him any details about what was going on, but the tension in the air reinforced Nestor's emerging sense of how serious it was. He adjusted his grip on his sword and felt his pulse throb against the grip.

They entered the theater as Laedan was jumped by the crowd. He made no effort to defend himself— not that it would have done much good. The mob pounded and stomped on him while Di Mon's cries fell on deaf ears. In the audience a woman screamed as another mob gathered around her. Di Mon threw people out of the way and slashed at anyone who tried to fight back as he made his way to Laedan.

Nestor ran to the woman in the audience, his black, red and white Nersallian garb shocking and frightening people enough that they stayed out of his way. When he made it to the woman, however, she was beyond help. Her face was a bloody mess and her body was spotted with red punctures. Nestor shook and spun around, waving his sword at the dishonorable cowards. They ran, tripping and stampeding over each other.

"Grab rats!" Nestor spat, gritting his teeth. He stood by the woman's corpse as though to protect it from further defilement, and tried to push away the image of his wife, Remei, replacing the woman on the floor. He shivered, for the first time shaken by scenes that reminded him of his family's safety— scenes that struck nerves from the Nesak war. Nerves he'd thought were already fried into cold apathy. Out of the corner of his eye he saw two children, a younger boy carrying a teenage girl, trying to get out of the chaos. Instantly an image filled his mind of his own son, Enid, trying to get away from the Caddy. He couldn't let it happen again.

Nestor's throat tightened and he dashed toward the children. He fought through the loud, dispersing crowd until he ran headlong into a messy fight between Di Mon's errants and angry citizens. Men punched, kicked and tore each other's clothing, the group pushed too close together to allow any of them enough space to draw a sword. It was three bloodthirsty men against two of Di Mon's— an unfair fight. Nestor slashed one of them in the leg, and they all spun around as though they'd only just become aware of anyone else in the amphitheater.

"Leave. Now," Nestor snarled.

A good look at his Nersallian jacket backed them down. It helped that Di Mon's errants were there beside him. Each man looked at each other, then the trio broke up and fled, leaving Nestor a clear path to the children.

The boy's face had a mixture of terror and anger twisted into a sneer Nestor hadn't thought possible on a child's face. The girl's eyes had gone to the back of her head and she shook violently. The boy struggled to support her and still maintain his threatening posture.

"It's all right," Nestor said, sheathing his sword. "I'm here to help you."

Di Mon's men were spreading out across the amphitheater floor, attempting to quell the rioters and protect their liege. There were several bodies that needed to be carried out, most of them dispatched by Di Mon. The rage still emanated from him in waves.

Nestor looked back at the boy whose face had transformed into an expression of deep sadness. Tears ran down the sides of his cheeks as he hugged his quaking sister to him, his lips trembling.

Gods, thought Nestor. *Was the mobbed woman your mother?*

Di Mon's errants were outnumbered. Arguments between them and the mob were getting louder. Some of the errants seemed unsure, themselves, about the rights and wrongs of the situation and were defecting to the rioters.

"Nothing more we can do here!" Di Mon called to Nestor and his errants. He ordered a withdrawal, his face betraying a hint of fear of the hysteria gripping the crowd. They tried to maintain the illusion of control and power but as they emerged from the amphitheater, Nestor carrying the girl over one shoulder and holding the boy in his other arm, they were halted by a re-forming mob.

"Abominations!" people shouted from the anonymity of the group.

Di Mon stopped and turned to confront them. "You will remember your place!" he demanded. "I am your liege!"

No one came within sword's reach of Di Mon and his following of Green House errants. For long seconds the tension prevailed, the air filled only by the sounds of heavy breathing and distant shouts.

"Let's go," said Di Mon, and pressed forward, sword in hand.

Nestor pulled the children closer to him as the girl stirred, knowing they had precious little time to get out before the chaos swallowed them. He followed behind Di Mon, his stomach twisted in worry over how to protect so many with so few. The crowd came to the same realization a moment later.

In a fluid movement that reminded Nestor of a pack of piranhas, the crowd separated him and the children from everyone else, forming a tight loop around him. Nestor ducked and set the children down, lifting his arms barely in time to avert the nearest attacker. He reached for his sword but couldn't move quickly enough. His head spun as he fell to the ground with the next assailant, and his vision blurred.

Chapter 3

Olivia awoke with her head spinning, sitting on the ground outside the amphitheater. Barely aware of her mental processes, she looked at the people jumping the man beside her and a protective impulse washed over her, from where she knew not. Her numbing cold grief turned into hot rage. With strength she didn't think she possessed, she shoved back a line of the encroaching mob and grabbed the ones who were on top of Nestor. What had happened earlier hit her in waves, and she let out a feral cry as she pushed through the crowd with Voltan and her rescuer. Later she would realize that it was her highborn strength, the gift from her murdered father, that had allowed them to escape.

When the three of them finally penetrated the outskirts of the crowd, they broke into a full run. Voltan couldn't keep up, so Olivia picked him up in her arms and began weaving into the surrounding neighborhood streets. The rescuer kept up to her at first, but she outran him, and ignored his cries for her to stop. The world had gone crazy and there must be a place — there *must* be — somewhere far away where everything was right. Where she could trade back her superior blood in exchange for a regular breakfast with her whole family. The thoughts served as *rel*-batteries as her legs pumped harder, running until lactic acid seemed to hiss in her ears and drown out all sound.

She ended up in a street with no cars, with the sun about to set.

Olivia gazed at the orange-red glow of the fading sun and turned to look at Voltan. His wide-eyes stared back at her, his brow creased with more lines than his years. She set him down beside her, heaving with the exertion of the last sprint. They said nothing to each other as they moved into a back alley and found a shadowy corner in which they curled up, knees pressed against their chests. Staring at the stain and grime caked on the alley walls, head spinning, Olivia's chest convulsed as she broke into sobs. She eventually noticed drops of Voltan's tears dotting the ground beside her.

Nestor peered into the tall, rich houses of the neighborhood, feeling suddenly very alien in a strange land. The houses seemed too quiet, the streets practically dead as his eyes darted around the green landscape that surrounded this small urban patch. People in parochial districts like Grianach, this far from big, cosmopolitan centers, were not known for their hospitality, and he expected none.

He knew the girl and boy had run off— likely as an extension of the fear and adrenaline that had coursed through them when the mob attacked, or as a coping mechanism after witnessing the murder of their mother. But if they were competent enough to elude him, did that mean they would make it on their own? They had clearly demonstrated highborn qualities by the speed at which they moved, something unusual for Monatese citizens but not impossible. Given the accusations shouted at them, he had an imprecise but strong sense that the children's abilities were tied up in the controversy that had left them orphans. Maybe they were something more than children. Something for which he had responsibility neither to help nor protect.

No, he thought, closing his eyes. *They were nearly killed back there. And so was I. We were lucky, and that luck might not stay.* Rubbing his thighs, he took a deep breath and set off at a brisk jog, not really sure how he would find them.

As he moved through the streets, Nestor wondered what the children would do. He wondered if they would be able to disguise themselves in another community, forever wary of the danger of being discovered. His guess was that they had been marked as outcasts by no action of their own and would probably pay the price for the rest of their lives. He couldn't help but think of Enid, his own son, who had grown up to be quite a recluse as a result of Nestor's unconventional choices. In his mind he could see both Enid and his wife Remei now, sitting in an uncomfortable hangar wait-ing for permission to enter the community. Di Mon likely had more important things to attend to right now, and it would be a while before they would see the green fields of Monitum.

Nestor made it to the outskirts of the town without see-ing anyone. Farmers' fields stretched before him, a wide foundation for the magnificent blue sky. The scene was soon marred by the sound of shouts in the distance, followed by a high-pitched scream. Nestor broke into a run, bashing through stalks of chest-high wheat.

Within a few minutes he was breathing flakes of wheat, and raised his head to see a grain extractor pursuing two small forms through the grass. Just as he got close enough to recognize the two children, the extractor went right over top of them.

Nestor screamed for the extractor to stop. But it just kept going. Frustrated, he tore out the wheat around him try-ing to shove away the world and get some distance from the ugliness. He wondered if the farmer had seen the two children, or, on the other hand, if he had purposefully gone for them. He fell to his knees and retched.

Pleo Ald'erda retreated with the mob as the Monatese guards threatened to slay anyone who continued the oppo-sition. He wanted to lash out, strangle, or maim anything within reach, but knew when to back down from an unfair fight. He'd managed to survive the wrath that had been unleashed on his mother, and he intended to live long enough to punish anyone who had played a role in his father's fall from honor. He would have to start at the space-port, where his father had worked. But he would need help.

Given how long the angry mob had defied the direct orders of the liege of the planet, he didn't think that was going to be a difficult task.

There was a loud bang, and the inferno of warring gods came alive on the ground. People screamed and scattered in all directions as the Monatese guards chased after the source of the noise.

"Gods, I wouldn't have gone that far," said a wrinkly-faced old man, clearly a commoner dressed in servants' clothes.

"Gone how far?" asked Pleo, turning abruptly. The cacophony in the air made him think of his mother's limp form, and he felt his heart pound faster.

"Use guns, my boy," replied the old man. "Committing atrocities to punish atrocities… it makes no sense." He furrowed his brow and bit his lip, before he began to hobble off away from the riot.

But how else can right win? Pleo asked himself. And smiled. The numbness that had covered his body was now tingling, and he thrilled at the opportunity for revenge. *Don't worry, Mom, I'll make things right.* As he ran off and escaped with the rest of the rebels, he started to laugh, his chest heaving until it hurt. No one heard him above the chaos.

Back at Green House, Di Mon's head throbbed and he felt like putting it into a vice, like one of the Old Earth torture devices. In the end, only a handful of people had been brought into custody. He felt a mixture of disgust and rage boil in his stomach. A large part of him wanted to capture and kill all the traitors who had disobeyed him and stampeded through his guards. On the other hand, he couldn't see how he could justify the slaughter of nearly an entire community, like a Nesak bent on religious purification. He sighed, picturing himself on the Challenge Floor, his true self discovered, exposed and punished just as cruelly as the Ald'erda family had been.

Rubbing his temples, he elected to go to the one place where people might try to escape: the spaceport. When he got there he was relieved to see his guards had maintained a strict perimeter, preventing anyone from entering or leaving. Roads in and out of the main town of Grianach had been sealed off earlier.

Several minutes later, Nestor's wife Remei and son Enid walked into his receiving room. Remei's auburn hair fell around her short face in waves, messy curls nearly masking her wary green eyes. She was dressed in a beige traveling gown. Enid's head rose just above his mother's hips, and his brown-haired head was lowered as he looked down at a furry form that he petted in his hands.

Di Mon stepped back in disgust. "Is that what I think it is?"

Enid's hand paused in mid-air, then he continued petting, his head not lifting. It was Remei who answered. "It's a Tarkian grab rat, Liege Monitum. A young one."

"Vile creatures," said Di Mon, clenching his teeth. It didn't look much like a grab rat to him, young or otherwise. He wasn't sure what it was and felt disinclined to speculate. "That thing has to go," he said.

"Go with us, Liege Monitum?" Remei asked with feigned innocence. "You have my word."

"I suppose arguing with you will be about as effective as it was with your husband," Di Mon said, turning away from them to look out the window at the idle space shuttles and planetary air ships on the sorting field where they would normally be organizing themselves for access to the runways.

"Less so," Remei assured him.

"Fine," said Di Mon, suddenly feeling tired. He turned to face them with a dark look on his face. "You are the only ones I'm letting enter this district, and that is based on the trust that I have for your husband. The situation is dire and any breach of my trust will result in the full force of my fury on everyone including," Di Mon pointed at the alleged grab rat, "your pet."

Remei put her arm around Enid and hugged him closer to her. "You can trust us," she said. "I knew you of all people would understand. People of Old Earth used to have pets of all kinds, as I'm sure you know."

"People of Old Earth used to slaughter each other in complete disregard of honor, reason or environment," snapped Di Mon, the images of the day's events cycling through his mind again. "Now get out." He barely refrained from adding, *Nesak!*

Remei's head moved backward as though she had been slapped, then she frowned and took Enid from the room. "Grumpy old goat," she whispered under her breath. "I don't know how Nestor puts up with him."

Chapter 4

Voltan sat in the harvester pressed up against his sister, staring at the pale-faced boy who was driving. The boy claimed to know his sister. His name was Faren, and he obviously had eyes for Olivia. He also upspoke them both, in the grammar of a Pettylord.

Voltan didn't like Faren. After all that had just happened, he wasn't going to let some stranger steal his sister away from him.

Faren tried to reassure them. "You'll be safe," he said. "My parents are in the city and won't be back for a while. I can make a bed for you in the barn where you won't be seen."

You're probably going to leave me in the barn and offer Olivia a bed in the house, thought Voltan. His scowl worsened. Despite himself, he was attracted by the idea of staying in a barn. He didn't want to spend any time with anyone right now, and wished he could run away — far away — and never speak to anyone again. He would take his sister, of course, and make sure she was all right. For now, however, a barn would do.

"I've seen you teaching some of the other kids," Faren went on, shuffling closer to Olivia on the seat as he drove. He looked her up and down. "You really have a way with them. I'm kind of jealous of how much they're learning from you." He added almost shyly, "About biology and things."

When Olivia said nothing, Voltan wondered if *he* was supposed to reply. He didn't think that learning was the reason for Faren's jealousy, and he again wished that Faren had run him over instead of picking them up with his harvester. At least there would be no more need to try to guess who could be trusted and who couldn't, in a suddenly hostile world.

"You must've had an awful day," Faren went on sympathetically.

Olivia finally snapped out of her trance, at least partially. "A little bit," she said.

"No more," said Voltan suddenly, his voice catching and sounding hoarse.

Faren's eyes widened as he shot Voltan a glance, but he said nothing. He remained quiet for the rest of the trip to his quaint home.

Voltan's first thought as they approached was that it was too clean for a farmhouse. The white exterior looked brand-new and the pathways in and out of the crops in the surrounding fields were outrageously neat. They walked up the steps to the front and Voltan felt each step get harder and harder as though hullsteel weights were added every time he lifted his feet. He groaned in a way that made him sound far older than his ten years.

Faren opened the door in a flourish, presenting the entry and adjoining living room as though they were the marvel of the planet. And again, Voltan thought that for a farmhouse, they were. The candlelit chandelier hung at the top of a high ceiling and homemade tapestries hung on the walls, reproductions of Old Earth Mongolian tapestry but nevertheless beautiful.

"Thank you," said Olivia, a hint of awe in her voice that seemed a feigned attempt to mask the pain she felt. Voltan wanted to tell her that she didn't have to hide it, but didn't know how to put it into words.

Faren led them on a tour, showcasing his mother's creativity and innovation when it came to decorating their household. Although his throat was dry and his stomach hurt, Voltan could appreciate the lack of wasted resources in comparison to some of the higher class households he'd been in over the years, growing up as a SeniorLord nobleborn. He added snobbery to the list of reasons why he didn't want to go back to society, on the off chance that people would actually accept them as highborn and force him to live as such.

"It's beautiful," said Olivia, barely louder than a whisper.

To Voltan's amazement, Faren displayed a bit of tact in his reply by not showing overexuberance. "We try to make do with what we have, and appreciate it."

After they had something to eat — the process revealing Voltan's ignorance with regard to food preparation without the aid of servants — Voltan was about ready to sleep. Despite the fact that he felt he should be protecting his sister, he fell asleep on a couch in the den at the rear of the house.

He awoke with Olivia shaking him violently, tears in her eyes while she spoke in a harsh whisper. "Get up!"

Voltan bolted upright as he heard Faren's voice down the hall talking to his father. From what Voltan had gathered on the way here, Faren's parents might not be too fond of having two freak shows sleeping in the den. He and Olivia darted out of the room into the kitchen, which was out of sight but not far from the main hallway. Under his breath, Voltan wished that Pettylord Sevolites had bigger houses.

"Supposedly the little rats are on the loose," said Faren's father, coming into the room where Olivia and Voltan had just been. "They're probably trying to get off planet where they could pass themselves off in somebody else's family, and make use of their highborn status," he grumbled in disgust.

"Yeah, probably," Faren agreed half-heartedly.

Faren's father's footsteps stopped abruptly. "Were you sleeping on the couch?"

"Um, yes," Faren replied. "I was so tired."

Faren's father stormed toward the kitchen. "I can't tell you how many times I've cleaned up after you. Your drool somehow gets on everything."

Voltan and Olivia darted out of the kitchen when they heard them coming, and were forced to move out into the hallway. Just as they started moving toward the door, a woman screamed and made them nearly jump out of their Monatese livery.

Faren's father came into sight. "What in the—"

Voltan and Olivia darted out the door and down the front steps. They heard cursing as Faren's father took off after them.

They ran into the fields that rose above their eye level and grabbed hands in order to keep track of one another. Hearing the harvester engine start up again, they tried to push themselves harder. Voltan felt sick to his stomach all of a sudden and vomited, the convulsions and muscle spasms too powerful for him to continue running. The sound announced their presence and he felt surrounded by the ugliness of the world in addition to the disgusting stench and sight of his meal on the ground and stalks around him.

For a moment, Voltan wished the harvester would run them over. Even after he stopped retching and the physical pain had waned, his chest ached and throbbed with echoes of the lonely vacuum his parents had once filled.

He looked up to see the harvester coming straight for them, and closed his eyes. A screech startled him and he saw that it had driven abruptly to the side, and he could hear Faren's father yelling at a woman who must have been Faren's mother. She jumped off the harvester into the tall grass and began running away, keys in hand. Faren's father cursed. "I'll deal with you later," he growled. He scanned the horizon for the children and Voltan shrank a little bit.

A ship descended low on the horizon, screaming closer to the ground than any Voltan had ever seen. It didn't seem to faze Faren's father, however, who approached him and Olivia with a purposeful and somber look, his sword slicing the grain as though it were a ship passing through cloud.

Olivia shouted, "We don't want any trouble. We've done nothing wrong. Please, let us go." She tugged on Voltan, but he heaved with the sudden movement, wanting to retch again. It was as though she had lit a spark in his brain by pulling on him, and all at once several images of the possible outcomes went through his mind. Faren's father running his sword through them, a mob coming out of the grain field and jumping on top of them, or their parents emerging from the ground to stop all the bad from happening.

The ship landed beside them hard and shook the ground in a teeth-chattering thud. It seemed to Voltan that between one blink and the next, a man jumped out of the airship, leapt through the grass and placed himself as a barrier to protect the children from harm. It was the man with the strange house colors and a dragon on his braid who had picked them up earlier.

"Who are you? Step aside," said Faren's father.

"This is the only chance you have to back down," the man replied in between gasps of breath. "Don't think I won't kill you to save these children."

"They're blasphemies," spat Faren's father. "The Watching Dead weep—"

The man pushed forward and hammered the sword out of the man's hands before striking him hard in the face. Faren's father crumpled to the ground. Voltan wondered if his own father, Laedan, had come back from the Watching Dead to save them.

The man turned to face the two tearful children, sheathing his sword with a ring that echoed into the emptiness of the surrounding field. Far off, Faren sprinted through the grass to try and reach them.

"You're not safe out here," the man said after a silence, stooping down to meet Voltan's eyes. "I can take you somewhere."

"No!" shouted Olivia, running up to the man and shoving him. He lost his balance and toppled. "Stay away from us." She laid a protective hand on Voltan's shoulder.

"I'm on your side, daughter of Ald'erda," Nestor said, propping himself up on an elbow wearily, his face a mixture of pain and pity. "I only wish to protect you."

"We don't need anyone's protection," she replied, bending to pick Voltan up. "We just want to be a family together." As she said the words, the image of Pleo in the crowded stadium came into her mind, and her mother's cries…

Her eyes rolled back into her head, and she fell to the ground, shaking, as a clear dream took over. She could see the murders happening in rapid repetition and the world became a sea of pain.

Their rescuer got up quickly and Voltan could tell by his expression that he wanted to help. In the instant Olivia had begun to clear dream, however, Voltan had bolted to her side, shielding his sister as his stomach continued to churn.

"I'm Nestor Tark," the rescuer said. "Son of Ald'erda, please let me help you."

Voltan held his quaking sister and wondered about the different passageways between *gap* that his father must have navigated in order to be reborn in Nestor.

"I'm Voltan," he said. Then he nodded, and looked down at his sister. She wouldn't be happy about this, but it was the best solution. That was about the only thing in the world that was clear to him.

The spaceport, normally bustling with activity, was dead, and Nestor had a hard time finding out where Remei and Enid had been sent.

Di Mon showed up and had Nestor summoned to meet him in a staff room. He was furious when he heard that he had brought the Ald'erda children with him.

"Have you gone mad? By all the gods, they are the primary focus of the hysteria," Di Mon said, angrily. He'd chosen to set up his office in a traffic control room, out of use now ships were grounded.

"I know that," Nestor snapped. "And I'm going to take them away from here, as soon as I get Remei and Enid."

"No!" Di Mon barked. "No one leaves. This atrocity could be the end of Monitum if anyone ever discovers what's happened. At the very least I'll have to retaliate even more brutally to prove I was not using science to solve Monitum's highborn problems."

Nestor exhaled heavily, looking at abandoned work-stations with the occasional family photos taped by the chairs. "You know I wouldn't betray you, Di Mon."

"It's not you I'm worried about."

"Olivia and Voltan are not safe here, and they may *never* be safe here," said Nestor, thinking of how long and hard Faren's father, and all those like him, would hunt until they found the children.

"I won't let them off Monitum," said Di Mon, his lined features more prominent than Nestor had ever seen. In the dim light it almost seemed like he was a commoner plagued by the tribulations of mortality.

That's what started this whole mess, thought Nestor. *Laedan wanted his children to be immortal.*

"That's good," said a throaty female voice behind them. "Because we're not leaving."

Nestor and Di Mon turned in shock to see Olivia, standing in dirty flight leathers with her dust-covered face lined with tear streaks that stood in sharp contrast to the resolve in her eyes. A shiny metal sphere hung around her neck and seemed the only clean thing on her body.

"How did you get in here?" Di Mon asked sharply, moving toward her.

She moved around the room just as quickly, eyeing the two men with suspicion. "I've lived here most of my life," she said, biting off her words. "We have a place here."

"Your parents owned the spaceport," Di Mon said, more to himself than anyone else, as he shook his head in self-chastisement.

"They still *own* it, and we're not going anywhere," said Olivia.

Nestor's features sagged when he realized he was out-numbered. He looked at Di Mon, hoping his friend and mentor would see reason.

"You're right, you're not giving up your inheritance," Di Mon decided. "But you're going to stay with Nestor until I sort this mess out, and not go parading around here waiting to be assaulted by the masses."

Olivia's nostrils flared as her arms tightened against her sides. "You think he can protect us? I snuck past all of your guards to get here. I can take care of my family better than you could ever hope to."

Di Mon twitched, then took a few steps toward Olivia. He took a deep breath. "I know you have suffered a tremendous loss today," he said slowly, "but I am liege of Monitum, and I need assurances from someone I trust that you are safe. Because," he lowered his voice, "there is far too much bloodlust in Grianach district right now."

"What about my mother's students? Who will teach them?" Olivia tried to make herself look tall, but ended up highlighting the fact that she was, in fact, still a child.

Di Mon's expression softened. "Your mother's peda-gogical habits were a beacon of light in the empire, and we will need light when this is all over. But until then such an act would only serve to put a spotlight on you and make it easier for the killers."

Olivia looked from one man to the other, her tightly-held expression of anger dissipating. "I still don't think he can handle us," she muttered, looking at Nestor.

As the offended Nersallian opened his mouth, Di Mon raised his hand. "Nestor will keep a much *closer* eye on you and Voltan than he has heretofore." He cast a sharp look in Nestor's direction.

Nestor tried to get a read on Olivia as they flew to a farmhouse on the outskirts of the province controlled by family Grianach. She hardly spoke, and Voltan seemed lost in thought. He tried to make small talk unsuccessfully. The trip continued in awkward silence.

The farmhouse they were heading for sat in a dip atop a rocky hill overlooking the valley, and was well-hidden from view below. Di Mon had recommended it and sent Nestor's family ahead to wait for him there. Nestor hoped Remei could make better headway with the Ald'erda children than he had.

Olivia scrambled out of her straps as soon as their little airship stopped moving, then helped Voltan out of his. Hand-in-hand, the two children strode to the front door of the small wooden house, ahead of Nestor.

Remei opened the door, Enid peering from behind her. Nestor felt an unconscious breath of relief escape from his lungs upon seeing that they were safe.

"Why, hello," Remei said happily, extending her arms. "You must be Olivia and Voltan."

"Don't think we're happy about this, lady," said Olivia, stopping a meter from Remei's arms.

"I understand," replied Remei. "I wouldn't be, either. Nestor can be a handful sometimes. Would you like some dinner?"

How Remei managed to agree with Olivia yet contradict her in the same breath, Nestor didn't know, but it worked. Nodding, Olivia went in, keeping Voltan close at her side. The boy kept his head down. Nestor followed along, keeping a distance so as not to break the spell.

When the children had gone into the kitchen, Nestor grabbed Remei's hand before she could follow them. "Thank you," he whispered, pulling her into a warm embrace. "You can't imagine what they've been through."

"I try not to," she said, kissing him on the cheek. Her hands went around his head, caressing him. "Right now they just need a safe place." She slipped from his grasp and moved quickly out of the room.

Enid came in clutching his pet takoshi in his hands, the costume to disguise it as a Tarkian grab rat still hanging off its shoulders. He and Remei had discovered the creatures in the Caddy's gambling fight rings, and Remei's sympathetic theft of one of them was the only positive outcome of the experience. Enid loved his pet Cam.

Nestor smiled. "Good to see you, big guy." He wrapped his arms around Enid's head and ruffled his hair.

"Is it true someone murdered their parents, Dad?" Enid asked, his voice soft and conspiratorial.

Nestor's expression sank a bit as he stepped back to look his son in the eyes. "Yes," he said, nodding and closing his eyes for a moment. "It is."

"Are they going to catch who did it?"

"I hope so."

Enid's brow furrowed. "What did they do that made everyone so mad?"

Nestor paused as the sickening reflection of what had occurred struck him in full force. The cries of Laedan and Sunniva, the children's mother, would be etched into his memory forever, and although he could understand the reasons why it had occurred, he couldn't see why it had happened in the manner it had. Mob violence wasn't what you expected on Monitum, a place that was generally more tolerant than other Gelack societies.

"Nothing," Nestor replied. "They didn't do anything."

Chapter 5

Di Mon, liege of Monitum, stared at the fields leading up to the principal city of Grianach, wondering if the clouds of dust were a sign of the turmoil that was going on, or merely the weather. He resisted the urge to pace in the small library of his regional office, because fury and frustration would take over if he started down that road.

"My Liege," said a slightly high-pitched, male voice. Di Mon turned to see Damek Kai'til in the doorway. He wore the green braids of Monitum on his sheriff's uniform and hunched a little bit as though the ceiling were too low. The Grianach deputy's black hair was short and tightly curled. His frame was tall and wiry. The uniform was a recent upgrade from deputy.

"You're late," Di Mon dryly.

"I came as quickly as I could," replied Kai'til. "There are too many attacks to keep track of."

Di Mon looked away. "The whole population can't have decided to stoop to such a level and disobey me without some sort of encouragement." Normally he would have been inclined to think everyone was behaving like an animal and look upon them with derision, but this time was different—this was Monitum.

"I don't know how it's being organized, my liege," said Kai'til, hunching forward more and shaking his head somberly. He wiped a sweaty brow. "Whoever's leading it is hiding better than a Tarkian grab rat."

"You should have enough errants to cover all of Grianach," said Di Mon sharply. He turned and took a step toward Kai'til, his fists shaking. "This needs to end."

"The mobs are not following *Okal Rel,* liege. They fight many on one, and are beginning to use poisons on their blades." Kai'til closed his eyes. "I've lost many of my finest swordsmen to gang-swords." He paused. "I'm surprised they haven't resorted to worse. But then, of course, illegal arms are hard to come by." He added, after a strategic pause, "Have you reconsidered escalating to military measures?"

"Keep it contained within Sword Law," said Di Mon.

The question made Di Mon wonder if he had made a mistake appointing the young but quick-learning Kai'til to replace the deceased Laedan as Sheriff of Grianach. But Kai'til was well-respected in the community and had the greatest chance of being able to reason with people he tried to apprehend. Di Mon wanted to stem the bloodshed as much as possible, which made Kai'til's job harder. He knew that someone was behind it all, though, and felt that punishing the puppets was the wrong course of action. Di Mon needed the puppeteer.

"You will have reinforcements," he said slowly, wondering how far he could afford to go before being forced to slaughter them all. It was a tricky business. If he came down too harshly on the rebels, he would be perceived as sympathetic toward the *okal'a'ni,* science-abusing, modified Monatese who'd tried to cheat the system.

Damn the Ald'erdas! thought Di Mon. It didn't help that Laedan has been his representative for upholding the peace under Sword Law before his downfall.

Kai'til allowed a grateful smile to cross his face. "Thank you, Liege Monitum. With more resources at hand, the faster we will find the phantom behind everything."

You better, thought Di Mon. "I will spend as much time as I can here," he promised. He wished that crises in the Empire could wait for one another, just take a seat in the waiting room like at an UnderDocks medical clinic. Then he wouldn't have to put his faith in an inexperienced youngster, however gifted he may be, and could handle it himself. But if Di Mon was missing from court too long, rumors might start and the risk of this event's exposure would increase. He put his palm on his forehead, touching his temples with thumb and forefinger.

"As treacherous as Ald'erda's acts were, he was a good leader," said Kai'til, breaking the silence. "I wish he were still here so that I could get his advice." He chuckled mirthlessly. "Then again, if he were here with his honor intact, we wouldn't be where we are, either."

Di Mon flinched. "No, we wouldn't," he said. He couldn't get angry with Laedan. He might have done the same thing to re-stock Monitum with highborns if it were safe. And socially acceptable. He would blame Gelack society's distrust of science, except for the many times history had proved such distrust justified. He frowned. He had to focus. Whoever had figured out how to modify genetics in an inheritable fashion was a force to be reckoned with, and he knew it wasn't the late Laedan Ald'erda. "Any news on the source of the... contamination?"

"No," replied Kai'til, shaking his head and hunching forward before straightening. He tended to bob slightly as he spoke, either up and down or from side to side. "The docks are owned by the Ald'erda family, and all records have been erased."

"Olivia," Di Mon muttered, gritting his teeth. "Or her mother." He shrugged. Which of them had done it didn't matter. "No trace of a shipment that might have contained anything of the sort?"

Kai'til shook his head. "Everyone who's injecting or injected seems to be two steps ahead of us. But there have been others. Not just Ald'erda."

Di Mon repressed a curse. He could feel the outbreak escalating into a pogrom. "Do you have any trace samples of the substance from the needles you have found?"

"Not yet, my liege," replied Kai'til. "The errantry are afraid to touch the stuff. I don't blame them."

Di Mon rolled his eyes. "Don't be stupid, Damek. If you could catch it like a disease, we'd all be infected." Upon seeing Kai'til's startled reaction, he added, "Then, I suppose, we could all kill each other."

"My liege, I hope—"

"Get out," snapped Di Mon, dismissing the young man with a wave of his hand. "You will have your reinforcements soon. Fleet *sha* trained in occupation tactics as well as duelists with appropriate local connections to satisfy the demands of Sword Law, plus operations staff and *gorarelpul* analysts. Come back when you have a drug sample to work with."

Sheriff Kai'til bowed and left the room as quickly as he could. Di Mon stared out the window lost in thought until the oranges and reds of a Monatese sunset layered the horizon. He wondered again, despite himself, if nature would continue its course as it had done before, no matter what happened to defile Monitum.

"It's a beautiful planet," said Nestor quietly, approaching him from the side. "You summoned me?" Nestor had hints of shadows underneath his eyes, and in spite of his highborn physique, he looked tired.

"Yes," said Liege Monitum. He turned and walked to a bookcase where he grabbed a book off the shelf and opened it to a section marked by a bookmark.

"You're going to tell me a story, my Liege?" asked Nestor. "Perhaps the children would appreciate it more."

Di Mon scowled. "You know, my Nersallian friend, there are few who can walk the thin line between irritating and useful as well as you can."

Nestor shrugged. "Lots of practice."

Opening the book and clearing his throat, Di Mon began. "There was an Old Earth story about a Goddess named Demeter, who presided over harvest. She was also linked to the cycle of birth, life and death. Some groups depicted her as Aganippe, a black-winged horse that destroyed mercifully. In either case, the people prayed to her so that the crops would be full and strong. She protected the green earth and its people. There was a man named Erysichthon—"

"I suppose we outgrew their fondness for impossible names," interjected Nestor.

"—who cut down a tree in a sacred garden which ended up killing a dryad."

"What's that?"

"Not important," said Di Mon, "but what is important is that Demeter punished Erysichthon by cursing him with insatiable hunger." He held up the book, where there was a black and white sketch of a man clutching his stomach next to a fallen tree. The dryad wasn't in the picture, but that was more than made up for by the exquisite anguish in Erysichthon's face.

Nestor cocked his head. "Are you worried that Demeter is going to descend on Monitum for the crimes it's incurring now?" Di Mon was not one prone to deity worship, as far as Nestor knew, and this religious metaphor worried him concerning his friend's mental stability.

"I don't know," Di Mon said quietly. "Monitum has always been a green haven with bountiful harvests. The Monatese have also been blessed with an appreciation for knowledge and rationality that few other Gelacks possess."

"Ahem." Nestor cleared his throat.

"I hold to my statement," Di Mon said with a glare. "We've seen the Nesak war. We've watched the Empire threaten to tear itself apart and yet the Monatese have managed to maintain a level of sanity separate from everything else in the reaches of the universe."

"Chaos has a way of finding its way into the smallest of gaps, Di Mon."

"That's just it, Nestor." Di Mon slammed the book shut. "What we are seeing is not chaos. Chaos does not inspire an entire district of citizens to rise up against their liege. Chaos does not provide organization to allow them to hide, to hunt, to maintain hatred over long periods of time. This isn't Erysichthon cutting a tree and accidentally killing a dryad. This is a planned targeting of the dryads." He exhaled and shut the book slowly, placing it back on the shelf.

"But who is planning it? Surely they would need some leader in the open, planning this for months. Laedan would have seen it."

"Maybe he did. Maybe that's part of the reason he was exposed and targeted," Di Mon said. "The worst of it all is that I can't see any of it. There's no trickle of evidence, no trail to follow." He bowed his head, a disgusted look on his face. "I can't see it all, Nestor. And I need a pair of eyes I can trust."

"You have them, my friend."

"It's all right— it won't bite," said Enid, opening his arms to Voltan, who sat pale-faced with his eyes locked on the Takoshi. "His name's Cam."

"Cam," Voltan repeated, lifting a quivering hand and slowly moving it toward the strange lizard. He wondered where such a thing had come from, and found his mind racing with the possibilities of genetic combinations that might result in its mutations. The forbidden stories and Lorel-influenced knowledge he had managed to salvage from various ships, either as gifts to his father or unwanted garbage, flashed through his mind as the lizard blinked at him.

He wondered if the lizard felt as strange, as lost in the sea of Gelack culture and contradiction as he did.

What anchors could a drifting soul ever find?

My parents are dead, he remembered.

He snatched his hand back before he touched Cam, and swallowed hard. Clutching his chest, he took in several heaving breaths and closed his eyes. Voltan wished he could be in anyone else's body, in anyone else's mind right now, and probably for the rest of time until the Watching Dead and the Living were one.

When he opened his eyes, Enid's were soft and sympathetic as he caressed the takoshi in his arms. Voltan blinked and looked around at the living room of the log cabin. The interior decoration consisted of small embroidered mats tracing separate lineages in cartoon-like images around the room. They only made him think of the short and incomplete nature of his own family's story.

There was nothing necessary about his parents' deaths. All at once, the pressure was too much to bear. He gave a yell and pressed his hands to his temples, tears pouring down his cheeks.

"What are you doing in here?" shouted Olivia, storming into the room. "Get away from him!" She knelt beside Voltan and wrapped an arm around him, glaring at Enid across the carpet.

"I was only trying to help," Enid said, bowing his head sadly. It wasn't the first time he had tried to connect with his new brother and sister, and the harshness of Olivia's rebuke hurt. He left the room in disappointment, carrying Cam the takoshi with him.

"It's all right, Voltan," said Olivia soothingly, running her fingers through his hair. "Everything's going to be all right."

"No," he replied.

Olivia fought her own instinct to agree with him. *He needs to believe it even if I don't,* she thought. "I know it's bad, but Mom and Dad are watching and are cheering us on, you know."

"I don't."

She tilted her head to look at him from the front. "Oh, and are you sure you'd be able to notice them if they were, given the way you're — how do you say it — intaking information right now?"

Voltan opened his eyes and let out a deep breath. "Maybe they've only come to see you."

Olivia's heart melted and tears welled up in her eyes. "Oh, dear brother, no. They loved us all— more than anything else. Dad only wanted the best for us, and did… what he did— with us in mind." The more she spoke, the more she wondered if she actually believed the words.

Voltan looked out the window. "Where's Pleo?" he croaked, his throat dry.

"I don't know," Olivia said, then continued in a whisper, "but I have a plan. Don't worry."

Voltan frowned. His mind began to churn again, calculating and estimating what his sister meant, and none of the results he got were good.

Nestor surveyed the scene and gagged at the stench of dead bodies. A family of three had been murdered in their own home. Their bodies were strewn with slashes outlining them like stick figures. There was blood everywhere, and somehow in this mess Nestor was supposed to find a clue as to how it all was happening under Sheriff Kai'til's nose.

The door didn't look as though it had been smashed in, so he reasoned that the victims may have known the perpetrators. He took his time looking at the door hinges, because it was a detail that was mundane enough and allowed him to look away from the gruesome scene. He had seen plenty of death in the Nesak war, but there was something altogether more cruel about these killings. Or maybe he had just pushed enough of the past behind him to forget.

When he turned around to face the room again, he realized what bothered him so much. It was the fact that the scene was not of a fight that had been lost — the people had been slaughtered. They lay in helpless positions on the floor, and there was no smashed furniture, or anything else to indicate a struggle had taken place.

"Find anything?" asked one of Kai'til's men, strolling in and standing beside him.

"It seems like they didn't put up much of a fight," said Nestor, covering his mouth and closing his eyes to regain control of his stomach.

"Maybe they couldn't, really," suggested the man, looking with disdain at the corpses.

Nestor stared. "I think anyone would fight for his life if attacked."

The man looked uncomfortable. "I just meant that maybe they were busy."

Nestor nodded slowly. "Maybe."

Screams pierced the ensuing silence. Nestor darted out the door and into the star-filled Monatese night. He waited for another sound to pinpoint the source of the noise, but there was nothing. The fields stretched off in either direction and he felt the emptiness expand out along with his helplessness.

"What have you been doing to stop the slaughter?" he snarled at Kai'til's man who now stood beside him. "Standing in the shadows and watching?"

"No less than what you've done," said the man.

Nestor closed his eyes. *I'll talk to Kai'til tomorrow,* he thought, *and find out how he's running his patrols.*

He turned back to go into the house, and said, "Get out there and rejoin your patrol. You're of no more use here."

"But what if they come back here, for you?"

"I welcome the challenge," said Nestor between gritted teeth. "With several of them it'll at least be a fair fight."

Chapter 6

Voltan heard a dozen whispering voices in his head, some softly singing soothing melodies while others muttered instructions at a volume just below his level of comprehension. He watched Remei bustling about the large kitchen as he sat on a stool at an island in the middle, and tried to concentrate on conversation.

"That school your parents ran sounds wonderful," said Remei, smiling at him. "You must've worked really hard. It shows."

Voltan wasn't sure how his intelligence or studious nature displayed itself to others, since as far as he was concerned he was going crazy and not doing much else. "Thanks," he said.

"What was your favorite book to read?" Remei pulled out a cutting board and plopped an onion on it.

"Anything to do with biology," he said, "or puzzles."

"Ah well, do I have a puzzle for you, young man," said Remei, pointing a bouncing finger of challenge at him. "It was one of the only clever things I learned from the priests on SanHome. It went like this:

"If my mother's sister is Lorel and her father is Vrellish on the day before a Demish wedding, what does that make me the week after?" She raised her eyebrows and began chopping the onion while glancing up at him.

"An impossibility or a liar," said Voltan without hesitation. "Either your father wasn't Vrellish, or your sister wasn't a Lorel. I don't see how the Demish wedding makes any difference."

Remei laughed. "Your answer is probably a lot better than the one the priests used to give. They would say, 'A genetic disaster.' I don't think they had a good sense of humor, or maybe they just liked to tell the Empire how important and sophisticated they were."

Upon seeing Voltan's stony-faced reaction, she flushed. "I'm sorry," she muttered. "It's… a horrible joke to bring up."

There was a rap on the door, and Remei dropped the knife on the floor, jumping to prevent it from hitting her feet. The rap repeated, so she picked up the knife and rushed out of the kitchen to see who it was. As she left the room, Voltan wondered where Olivia was, and whether ignoring him was part of her grand plan to re-unite the family. The conversation he had just had with Remei was probably about the longest one he had had since… it happened.

"Please," said a panting, rough voice from the other room, "you must let us stay here. It's the only place they won't search."

"Who won't search?" Remei asked.

"The Sheriff's' men."

Remei's voice trembled as she spoke her next words. "Wh— why are you running from them?"

Voltan hopped off his stool and edged around the corner of the kitchen, getting a view of a dirty man in tattered clothes with a mix of blood and soot covering his face. The man looked confused, as though running away were not really a choice. "They're trying to kill us," he said.

Remei's face turned white. "And who are you after?" she asked quietly. Voltan saw her grab a wooden baton that stood tucked behind a dresser in the front entry. He started breathing heavily and quickly, fearing the worst was about to happen.

"Your Grace, we are after no one," said the man, a tired expression crossing his face as his shoulders sagged. "By all the gods, we did nothing wrong. They say we are heathens, outrages, tainted ones. But how different are we from you? You… you harbor changed ones here? Don't you?"

Remei stared at the man, afraid to admit she did and unwilling to reject him, either. He stared back, equally undecided. Until all at once something relaxed in him and he drew a hand gun from beneath his jacket to offer it to up to Remei in shaking hands.

"Look," he told her. "See what they are using against us?" He searched her eyes as she stared at the weapon in horrified disgust. It was a sure sign of "the first step". The harbinger of unlimited violence. Mass destruction.

"It is Kai'til's men who commit abominations," the man said, holding up the vile gun, like an offering.

Remei let go of the baton in her hand. "Oh Gods," she said. "What is Kai'til doing? Come in, quickly."

She snatched up the offered gun as if it were red hot, and hid it quickly in her clothes.

Voltan shrank into the corner as the man beckoned his friends in with him, and soon the house was bustling with people who were supposedly much like him in the sense that they were afflicted by the same modified blood. Nevertheless, Voltan sat alone in the corner the rest of the night.

Olivia clutched Faren's hand and tugged him through the night streets of Texeba, the capitol city of Grianach. She let go once he was beside her, and she made a sharp indication with her finger against her lips to keep quiet. They peered around the corner at two of Kai'til's men who had crossed paths while on patrol.

"Any mold on your route?" said the taller one.

"Nah, the place's been cleared out."

"What about a drink?"

At that, the shorter one grinned, reaching into his trousers to pull out a bottle. The taller man cheered, and they began passing the bottle between the two of them. Behind stood a tall factory where grain was turned into flour, and where both Faren and Olivia thought that the vigilantes might be hiding. She swallowed, grateful that Faren had tracked her down and agreed to help her find Pleo.

"Come on," she whispered, and they darted across the street as the two guards smacked each other on the back in exuberant good humor. She and Faren made it into the other alley and peered into the only window at ground level.

They saw a sleeping guard in an office. Olivia grinned mischievously at Faren, who shook his head in objection. She opened the door quietly, snuck past the desk and opened the door behind the guard. Widening her eyes at a fearful Faren, she watched him tip-toe in and nearly bump into a bookshelf on his way over.

The dark hallway beyond was lit by a single lamp, and at the end was a creaking door that made Olivia wince as she tried to open it.

"We can go back," whispered Faren, looking over his shoulder.

"No," said Olivia, turning on him. "I know they're keeping prisoners here. It's the only place big enough to house them without being seen. They might have Pleo."

She watched Faren bite his tongue, and tried to ignore the same thought that was crossing her mind. *I'm not sure they are taking prisoners.* She closed her eyes and quivered, her chest aching as she fought off a slip into a clear-dream. *If any of them knew what this was like,* she thought, *they'd know we are cursed already.*

Opening her eyes, her expression hardened and she turned back to the door, disregarding Faren. She pushed it open, her muscles moving so slowly she had to remind herself that she was using them at all. The way her heart was pounding, she wanted to shove the door open. She could feel her muscles pushing her in that direction, encouraging her to lash out. She wondered if that was her highborn physique starting to kick in. *I might need it on the way out.*

Any sound the door may have made was drowned out by the cries and shouts below. The dank walls had moss growing down like a vegetal waterfall leading deeper into the underground cavern below the factory. The staircase was uneven and as Olivia and Faren crept toward the few lights far below, they could see more and more shapes in the shadows.

"To our newest members," said a booming voice, "do you swear to eradicate the mold?"

Cheers flew up and several people stepped forward or were shoved into the light below. Olivia motioned for Faren to stop and they perched atop the scene on the craggy staircase. She recognized a few of the people who had come forward— some had been regular patrons of the spaceport.

One was a short, stout man who had always been keen on taking her father's position.

She nearly yelped when she caught herself biting her lip too hard.

A younger man stepped forward, taking a few measured, echoing steps that drowned out all sound in Olivia's mind. *No. NO.*

Pleo Ald'erda joined the crowds of the newest inductees into Kai'til's gang of mold eradicators, and looked around with a wolfish and predatory gaze, his eyes narrowed.

Olivia opened her mouth to scream but Faren's hand covered it, and she saw the world spin around her as images flicked into her mind of the honeybees in the forests to the North, the furry quadrupeds of an Eastern region, and then suddenly a battlewheel en route to Monitum, towering like a harbinger of death that would come soon if the planet didn't consume itself, first.

She opened her eyes as shouts escalated to a deafening cacophony, and dozens of gang members charged up the stairs toward her and Faren. They drew their swords, which were shorter than regular dueling swords: weapons suited for easy access and mobility, for slaughter.

Faren reached for Olivia's necklace and tugged hard, snapping it off its chain and making her stumble forward. "Get back!" he shouted, holding up the heavy Old Earth necklace as though it were an explosive weapon. "Or you will all die."

The strange, carved metal ball certainly looked like it might be something dangerous, and the men stopped in their tracks. They whispered amongst themselves, and Faren cut them off. "Let us leave and no harm will come to you."

"He's bluffing!"

"Get them!"

The attackers continued up the staircase, and Faren made a bit of a show of pretending to ready the device, but his hands were shaking.

"Stop! He's telling the truth," came Pleo's voice far below. "I've seen that *okal'a'ni* weapon before. Keep back! Let them leave."

Olivia wanted to kiss her brother, and she felt a little sunshine radiate on the hole in her heart. She stood up, still shaking on her feet and seeing frightening images at the edges of her field of vision. She began climbing the stairs as Faren walked sideways behind her, keeping an eye on the gang.

The moss on the walls seemed to jump out at Olivia, and she wondered if the gang intended to clean their hideout as the first step to getting rid of human mold. *May they never find you out, dear Pleo,* she thought. Although she still couldn't understand why Pleo was with them, she knew he would never betray his family.

When they reached the front entrance the guard jolted awake and made a motion to get up. Faren punched him hard in the face, stunning him before he and Olivia ran out. Rain spattered the ground as they disappeared into the night.

Chapter 7

Nestor walked on dirty pavement, scraps of clothing blowing about in the wind as though everyone had been trying to leave a fabric trail to follow. The village was barren, and the wind whistled, eerily, between the buildings. He jumped at the slightest sound, mistaking wind gusts for whoops and jeers of the gang that he knew existed only by what it had left behind in its wake.

Store fronts had been smashed and looted, the less useful items left strewn about the street. Nestor could see dried blood spatters here and there on the pavement, and could smell the stale stench of sweat as he went farther in.

If entire villages are deserted, he thought, *how many people have modified themselves? The people of Monitum don't trust science that far, do they? Not enough to justify any significant amount of drug being passed around in an effort to gain blood rank for one's family. Maybe the killers aren't being very discriminating.*

He noticed a larger clothing shop that looked less vandalized and even had a working door that blocked the view to the inside. Drawing his sword, he walked over, careful to avoid kicking any of the debris that would announce his presence.

When he reached the door, he pushed it open slowly. A man yelled and nearly speared Nestor in the face. Nestor lurched back in time, seeing the reflection of his eye off the side of the blade. Nestor lined up and put all of his weight into kicking the door in. He could immediately see a family cowering in the far corner and the man, dirty and disheveled with bloodshot eyes, growled at him.

"You'll never get them, you coward!" he said, quaking in anger. He looked old like many citizens off Monitum, since none were naturally highborns. "You forget the power of belief and honor that all you rats lack!" he railed at Nestor.

"Calm yourself, friend," said Nestor, shrinking down and backing up to indicate neutrality. "I didn't come here to hurt anyone."

"I've heard that before," replied the man, glaring icily. He looked Nestor up and down. "Although you don't have the same garb as the ones who are shaming Monitum."

"I'm here to hunt the killers down," said Nestor, sheathing his sword. "And protect those they seek to harm. It looks like we have the choice of fighting, or of taking a leap of faith that the other is not lying."

The man shook his head and pointed with his sword. "I'm feeling generous, so go back where you came from and I'll let you live."

A chorus of chanting sounded in the distance, echoing into the thin walls of the shop. Nestor turned sideways and peered into the street, keeping the old man in the corner of his eye. There were a group of Monatese soldiers running in formation toward the village, and Nestor breathed a sigh of relief. He had never heard of them chanting songs together, but if that meant they were doing a better job of protecting Monitum's citizens, he didn't care.

"You drew them to us!" hissed the man, charging Nestor.

Nestor jumped to the side, slamming himself against the wall to dodge the man's blade. He waited for the opportunity, planted a kick in the man's chest and drew his own sword. A few seconds later he intentionally locked the hilts of their blades together, and gripped the man by the shoulder. "I'm on your side," Nestor said. "And the sheriff's troops are here to help you."

"Are you space drunk?" said the man, his lips quivering in fear. "Kai'til's running the slaughter."

Nestor's jaw dropped and he let go of the man. He motioned to speak but couldn't find the words. There was no way the man was lying— not from the look on his face. The tromping footsteps of the squad drew closer.

"Go," said Nestor. "Run. Take your family and run. I'll hold them off."

"There's at least twelve of them," said the man, unlatching his sword from Nestor's. "You won't make it."

"Don't worry about me. I hold some authority over them which may give me some time." Nestor grabbed the man's shoulder and pushed him away. "Now go!"

The man muttered in bewilderment as he stumbled back in to pull his wife, two daughters and son from the back room. They raced down the street as Nestor strode out to meet the approaching squad.

"Halt!" Nestor commanded, standing tall and brandishing his sword. He could feel his pulse rise up in his throat as though his heart no longer wanted to follow mind and body. He tightened his sword grip.

The platoon slowed in front of him, and the tall, black-haired leader glared at him. "You let the mold slip from your grasp, friend Tark. A little too easily, I might add."

"Mold? Is that what you call them?" Nestor said, lifting his sword to sweep it before the Monatese men and women. "Then that would make you what, plant poison?"

The leader smiled mirthlessly. "Something like that. I guess the question is which category you fit into." He looked back at his troops, who were sneering. "It was always surprising, how close Di Mon kept you even though you were Nersallian. I heard you married a Nesak, to gain a *rel*-bride. So your children would be Royalblood. Maybe you even *started* the mold that is growing in Grianach, from your obsession with Nesaks."

The soldiers whooped and broke apart, beginning to form a circle around Nestor. "Have you gone mad?" Nestor said, unmoved in the center. "I haven't the intelligence for such a thing, even if I wanted to do it."

"Of course," said the leader, cocking his head. "Yet you still help them."

"I will protect anyone who's innocent," said Nestor, leveling his gaze at the men around him. "And that excludes you." He stabbed his sword into the foot of the man closest to him, causing the man to bend forward in pain. In a split second Nestor leapt up onto the man's back and out of the circle, sprinting away down the street.

"After him!" yelled the leader.

Nestor didn't know how narrowly he had missed being maimed, but didn't care to look back, either. He ran in the opposite direction the family had fled, praying to the gods he wouldn't run into more of Kai'til's troops.

I have to tell Di Mon, he realized.

Pleo Ald'erda fought to maintain control of himself, his hands shaking as his fellow warriors looked at him in confusion where he knelt on the ground in the dim light of Monitum's setting sun. The butchered corpses of several identified abominations lay scattered in the rural village around them, the grass turned brown by sunbaked blood. Pleo relished what he had done, or at least his mind did. His body, on the other hand, seemed to remember his berserk episode with horror, and he gritted his teeth as vivid images of blood-spatter flashed in his mind and turned everything red.

He came to himself in the midst of an argument among the men and women he had fought beside. Drool coated his cheek and he tried to straighten himself as he pushed to a seated position, feeling disgusted at his demonstration of weakness.

"There's never been a Monatese who's freaked out like that."

"He must be an abomination, too!"

"No! He's one of us! He's Pleo!"

Pleo couldn't tell who was speaking, but a sense of fear grew in him like fractures splitting across a frozen lake. His awareness snapped back and his vision came into sharp focus. There was his friend Sigurd who seemed to be arguing for Pleo's salvation, and the leader, Annona, who thought he should be killed alongside the villagers.

"He's shown he's on our side," Sigurd said, throwing an arm up in Pleo's direction emphatically. "How could he be one of them and still kill them?"

Pleo knew exactly how, and he knew Sigurd did, too. He had noticed Sigurd go into a berserker's trance on some of their marches through diseased villages. He, like Pleo, was a modified citizen, an "artificial" highborn.

"He's a spy," said Annona flatly, looking at Pleo with murderous eyes amid her sharp features. "That's how he could do it." The squad closed in on him and the sun seemed to hasten its descent below the horizon.

Pleo drew his sword and spun in a wide arc that slashed the shins of all the warriors surrounding him. An instant later he was on his feet and pushing past them. He cried out when a blade nicked the back of his shoulder, and he heard the footsteps and shouts close behind him. The injury seemed to intensify his focus, however, and he ran faster than he ever had before. He wondered if it was his highborn gifts that had allowed him to escape, and hated himself for it.

He ran until the ground became rougher and he could no longer hear anything but the throb of the Monatese earth, ashamed with each step he took upon it. When he came to the outskirts of a neighboring village that looked as waylaid as the one he had just left, he slowed to a walk.

There were no words for anything, and he struggled, muttering to himself and growling angrily when nothing came out right. He found a corner of an abandoned and looted sword shop and sat down, holding his head between his knees and pressing his palms against his temples.

Who were they to cast judgment? It wasn't like they knew what it was like. Pleo *did*, and wondered how something like what he was experiencing could ever have been mistaken as an advantage. Kai'til's pawns judged him as though he had a choice in the matter. He was highborn, but *he* hadn't committed anything *okal'a'ni* to be that way.

The killing was a need. A compulsion. The only thing that started to bring calm, if only temporary.

He felt a pang of guilt for the children they had killed during their afternoon crusade, and shouted in frustration over how stupid he had been. The real criminals were the adults, the people who had made the decision to self-modify in the first place. He wondered how many of Kai'til's men had modified their own children and were playing executioner hypocrites to cover up. They were too many of them, though, for him to fight, and he pounded his fists against his knees as tears poured down his face.

A creak at the front of the store made him freeze into silence. He picked up his sword, hand trembling, wondering how he could fight his way out of a corner.

"Pleo?" said a familiar, boyish voice.

Pleo edged out until he could see that Sigurd was alone. "Where are the others?" he asked.

"Far from here, but aside from that I'm not sure," Sigurd replied. He took in deep breaths and leaned forward, resting his arms on his knees.

Pleo walked through the vandalized counters and tables to reach his friend. "Why didn't you stay with them? They're going to assume you're with me, now."

"I *am* with you, Pleo," said Sigurd, straightening himself proudly. "They would have found me out eventually, too."

Pleo's fists clenched and quaked with rage. "They haven't the foggiest notion of what it's like to wake up and be a disgrace to everyone and everything," he said loudly. "As if we chose this life."

"They're rats, the lot of them," agreed Sigurd.

"The only people we should harm, Sigurd," said Pleo, leveling his gaze, "are the ones who modified *themselves*. Who chose to curse their children."

Sigurd frowned, then nodded. "They caused this whole mess."

"Yes," Pleo said, his pulse quickening. "And there are many more of us out there. We've already seen how many more people have modified than anyone would have ever expected. We have to rescue other kids like us, and when there are enough of us, we can fight back."

Sigurd's eyes lit with excitement. "Yes!" He paused, as if surprised to discover hope in so much despair. Then he exalted, louder, "Yes, yes!"

They grinned at each other as any two boys who are about to go on an adventure together. For the first time since he had discovered the curse of his modified blood, Pleo felt accepted and hopeful. Here was a course of action he could take stock in, and guide to see it through to full justice.

Mom would be proud, he thought.

Olivia had been astonished to find the house full of refugees when she returned from her excursion with Faren, and was overwhelmed by the number of people who were content to be crammed into the space of a closet if it meant safety from Kai'til's forces. She had found her bed and collapsed until late the next morning, when she went down for breakfast.

"Where's Voltan?" she asked Remei, having to shout above the cacophony of voices in the dining room. All around her there were people whose clothing had been torn through fighting or fleeing, some with blood stains that were a few days old. They had run away with the clothing on their backs, and nothing else. The room reeked of sweat and Olivia found herself wishing she was on Golden Demora.

"What?" yelled Remei. Her hair was unkempt and she moved about briskly, giving out tea, biscuits and anything else she had to offer.

"Where is my brother?" Olivia repeated, before she was jostled out of the way by a troupe of hungry boys. Remei still didn't hear her, and the room was too crowded now to have any conversation.

"You welcome the entire world, but you won't help me find my family," she said bitterly.

"Sorry?" said Remei.

Olivia shook her head, acknowledging that words were no longer useful.

She went upstairs to the bedroom, and found Voltan curled up laying sideways with a book. Heaving a sigh of relief as she closed the door and approached him, she asked, "Whatcha intaking?"

He didn't turn to look at her. After a pause, he said, "A myth about the Old Earth gods."

She furrowed her brow. "Really? I thought you didn't believe in that stuff."

"I don't," he said, still facing the wall with his book open.

"Then why are you reading it?"

"The people in the stories all had a connection to something much greater than themselves," he said slowly, biting his lip. "That was what religion meant to them— being connected with something outside of their own interests."

Olivia nodded, not fully understanding what her brother was getting at. "Like our connection to the Watching Dead?" she suggested quietly.

"Better than that," Voltan said. "For them, the connection was real. They weren't just pretending."

She gave a small gasp, as though her brother had just denied the existence of their parents. "You don't mean that."

Voltan was quiet, then said, "Where have you been?"

Olivia was about to say *Looking for Pleo* but stopped herself. Voltan would want to come with her and she didn't want to risk his life in the increasingly violent streets of Grianach District. She couldn't come up with an adequate excuse. "I've been ... busy ... helping Remei get crops to feed everyone."

Voltan said nothing, and Olivia glanced at the clock in the upper corner of the room. She had promised Faren that she would meet him again in the late afternoon, which was quickly approaching. Her heart sped up when she anticipated the encounter, and she found herself smiling.

"Listen, I'll be back later, okay?" she said, touching Voltan's shoulder. He nodded, moving his face closer to his book.

"That sounds like a neat book," she went on. "I'll have to read through it when you're done."

"That'll be soon," he said.

She grinned. "Of course it will, you little genius."

She hurried out and found the bathroom, where she unpacked her bag with a beautiful green dress she had found in one of the ransacked shops. It was a bit impractical to conduct stealth work, but it was *so pretty.* In the middle there was a brooch that seemed to hold everything together, with fabric lines that ran radially outward from it. The folds of the dress made her want to lose herself in the smooth linen that felt so comfortable. It might have been simple by Demish standards, but she loved it.

Slipping into it, she tested putting her hair up or leaving it loose over her shoulders. "Okay, fine," she said, her practical side getting the better of her as she tied her hair into a ponytail. She flicked her hair over her shoulder and tried to giggle flirtatiously. *I'm ridiculous,* she thought, straightening. *These jaunts aren't for dates.*

Nevertheless, she continued prettying herself up for at least half an hour, and by the end of it she had convinced herself that she was, in fact, as pretty as a Demish princess. It was a wonderfully unfamiliar feeling, and she twirled once to get a view of herself at all angles. Why couldn't she be a princess? For the second time that day, she wanted to move to Demora.

"You look good," said Voltan's voice beside her, making Olivia jump in surprise.

"What are you doing here?" she snapped, folding her arms across her chest in an attempt to conceal her appearance. It was the first time in her life that she had ever felt *pretty* and Voltan had invaded her privacy.

"I— I just—"

"Get out. Now," she said, pointing a damning finger at the bathroom door.

"I just wanted to tell you about—"

"Did you not hear me the first time? Screw your head into the world for a second. I want to be alone."

Voltan's gaze fell to the floor and he turned around slowly, slinking out.

"Oh come on, you can't pout forever," she said, rolling her eyes. Waiting until Voltan was out of sight, she checked her appearance once more, and realized that she had lost the beatific look from before. Wrinkles of worry and anger lined her forehead, and she tried to smile innocently, to no avail. Glancing at the clock, she cursed as she realized that she would be late for Faren, who should be waiting at their usual meeting spot.

Pushing her way through the crowds downstairs, she nearly fell out the front door. After picking herself up from a near-trip, she began to sprint. Almost immediately, a hand grabbed her and she toppled to the ground.

"Olivia!" Faren said, worry covering his face.

She was about to ask him why he had come up the hill when she caught sight of the road behind him. It was filled with troops who marched and chanted. They blocked all passage and stretched down the hill out of sight.

"Oh gods," she said with a gasp, wondering briefly if Pleo was among the troops. "They've found us."

Chapter 8

Voltan lay curled on his bed, pressing his hands against his ears in an effort to keep out the continuous clamor of the house. His mind raced with the possible things his sister was doing, all of which infuriated him. Several minutes later he felt guilty for being so possessive and self-entitled to his sister's attention, which just made him feel worse.

I'm not that demanding, he thought, his lips quivering in the waning light coming through the window. *I don't ask for that much, do I? Why do I have to force people to care?*

He pounded his fists against the bed, groaning.

Nestor had appeared as though he was the reincarnation of Voltan's father ushered in to save the day and make everything normal again.

But you've forgotten us, he thought miserably, thinking of how many times he had tried to talk to his surrogate father unsuccessfully.

Enid had been kind, but when the refugees came both he and Remei were far too busy to pay attention to him.

Voltan felt like he'd been rejected and was kept in the house only out of pity.

He needed to tell someone about his constant stream of thoughts. It was more than just restlessness. It was as though his enjoyment of puzzle-solving had intensified to a need, and everywhere he looked he tried to fit things together in his mind, or rearrange them into a more logically pleasing configuration. He wanted to shut it off, and had tried with several books and games in an attempt to distract himself. It wasn't working.

Maybe his father had come back in the form of someone else, outside of Grianach. Why would it even be limited to that? His father might be growing up in another reach, in a zone where no Gelack had ever gone before. The thought made Voltan smile, imagining his father as a pioneer in some far-off land.

Shouts from downstairs shook him from his reverie, and he scowled as his mind seemed to pulse faster and faster with images of *rel*-ship flying patterns, docking procedures, maps of the major reaches and constellations. All things his father had shown him at one time or another, but running together, demanding, and out of control.

I can't take it, he thought, trying to talk back to the involuntary flow before it got out of control. *No, please, no.*

He stood up abruptly and clenched his shaking hands as he headed down the hall to Enid's room. The noise was so loud downstairs it seemed like there was a party going on. Voltan opened Enid's drawers and began stuffing clothes into a bag. Enid was slightly larger and taller, but the clothes would do well enough.

Voltan opened the window that looked out at the backyard and looked out on the remainder of the grassy slope before the hill took a sharp downward turn. He took a deep breath. His mind flew ahead to the spaceport, then came flying back to reality. He began climbing out the window, lowering himself onto the ground.

If he kept moving, he might be able to outrun his mind.

Remei heard the front door slam and Olivia's shrill voice pierce the background noise of the kitchen. "Kai'til's mob is here!"

She froze as screams broke out and everyone began to jostle for safety, or for a look at what was approaching them. Remei couldn't move even if she wanted to, and she wondered desperately where everyone thought they would escape to. They were all stranded and easy targets in a neatly packaged container for the slaughter.

I'm so foolish, she thought, as someone shoved her to the side and she nearly smashed her face into the counter. She thought about the gun sequestered on her person. Ever since she'd taken it, she'd felt its weight like a brand of shame. Now it felt like hope. But if she used it to defend them, wouldn't she invite a slaughter? Did she even know how? She had to trust its previous owner had left it ready to use.

Even this thought frightened her, for fear it was supposed to be put into a sleeping state to make it safe for carrying, in secret, on her person.

"Please keep calm!" she shouted.

As menacing jeers began to join the background noise, she began trembling. "Enid! Enid!" Remei cried. "Where are you? Voltan! Olivia! Enid!"

Pleo and Sigurd lay on their stomachs in the grass and watched as the mob began to fan out around the house.

"No," cursed Pleo, gripping the short-bladed sword he clutched beside his breast. "They won't get you, Olivia, I promise."

He stood up and started running toward the house. A few of Kai'til's men saw him, but they hadn't been there when he had been tossed out. They thought he was charging the house, and when he ran one of them through with his blade, the other was too slow to react before he fell, too.

Pleo's heart thudded in his ears, the edges of his vision red as he made sure the two men weren't getting up. His highborn strength was coming in handy. "Come on!" he shouted at Sigurd. "We have to save them!"

He ran to the back of the house, and began climbing the trough that he had spied after he had followed Olivia home the night she had nearly been caught. The pipe shook as he shimmied up, and some sharp edges in the metal cut his hands. He climbed in through the window, and found a trembling boy who shouted and backed into a corner, clutching a strange-looking creature in his hands.

"Relax," said Pleo, scanning the cramped room quickly. "Where's Voltan?"

"Gone," said Enid in a quavering voice. "I— I don't know where he went."

"Aren't you supposed to be taking care of him?" snapped Pleo. He pushed into the hallway where he saw a throng of people surging toward him. Quickly, he stepped back into the room and slammed the door. He knew that there was precious little time before the mob started mowing through the house.

"What about Olivia?" Pleo asked.

"She was trying to lead people out," Enid said. "I came up here to grab Voltan, and…" His voice tapered off.

"Gods," Pleo muttered, biting his lip. *Olivia can handle herself*, he concluded after a moment's thought. "All right, you're coming with me."

"What? No," Enid said, brow furrowed. "I don't even know who you are."

"I'm Pleo, Voltan's older brother," he answered, then his face curled into a sneer as he lifted his blade. "And yes, you *are* coming with me."

Cam, the takoshi, growled in Enid's hands, but Enid silenced him with a hand around his muzzle.

"Oh— okay," Enid said with a gulp.

Pleo led Enid through the back window and out of the chaotic struggles that now filled the house. No one seemed to notice them.

The panicking refugees shoved Remei against the hall-way wall as they pushed upstairs. She heard the taunts from outside as Kai'til's soldiers surrounded them. Trembling, she looked at the closed front door — wood-trimmed and carved with Earth flora and fauna — which right now seemed like the gateway to Hell.

Swallowing, she stepped toward it and gripped the handle. Her hand no longer felt attached to her as she pulled the door open and her limbs went cold.

The yelling stopped for a moment as the leader silenced the attackers. "An abomination has opened the door for us," he said, eliciting whoops and cheers from the crowd.

"I'm not an abomination," Remei said loudly, hoping her voice sounded braver than she felt.

"Right," said the leader. "But you harbor them."

"There are no abominations here," Remei said. "You might have better luck elsewhere."

The crowd roared in anger, making Remei wince, clench-ing her fists to store up the courage to continue standing there.

"I've seen the refugees clumping in here," the leader said, tracing a circle around the house with his sword. "If you are not one of them you'd best step aside."

"No one is going anywhere," Remei went on. "But while you're here for a visit, why not come have some food?" She tried her best to make the invitation sound sincere.

The leader howled with laughter. "You think some dried pheasant and bread are going to deter us? We walk in the path of righteousness, traitor, and will stem the tide of darkness that threatens to engulf Monitum."

"Darkness? You're perpetuating it!" shouted Remei, unable to hold back her tongue. "These people have no intention of hurting anyone else."

"Enough of this nonsense," said the leader, sensitive to the growing unease amongst his troops. He turned to them. "You can't reason with traitors— their mouths speak nothing but lies and deceit. And if we do not cauterize our shame before Liege Monitum's reinforcements get here, all the empire will know of it and our liege, himself, will pay with his blood on the challenge floor!" He gave a wave of his arm, and the men charged.

Remei lifted her arms in surrender, her face set in a grim, determined gaze. "May your true souls return one day," she said, her Nesak teachings flooding her thoughts instinctively. In a few seconds, it would all be over. They could not win. They were not warriors to rally and stand against assassins. But would she pull the gun to fight back, sullying her soul on the brink of death, or die hiding it?

A red figure leapt through the air and impaled the warrior closest to Remei, an animal cry piercing the sky. Nestor tore his sword out and kicked the warrior behind him, fending off attacks from all sides as Kai'til's angry militia swarmed him.

"Nestor!" shouted Remei when she saw one of the soldiers leveling the barrel of a gun at him. The bullet sounded but Nestor kept fighting. Not intending to give them a second chance, Remei pulled her own, illicit handgun out of the back pouch of her dress and lifted it, holding it steadily.

"See! They use *okal'a'ni* weapons!" one of the soldiers shouted, evidently unaware of the hypocrisy.

Remei squeezed the trigger. The soldier with the gun fell, and some of the warriors around Nestor wavered long enough for him to dispatch one of them. Remei aimed again.

"Get her!" shouted the leader, standing at the back of the mob. A horde of angry Monatese was already headed for her, and she fired again.

As one man was nearly upon her, a green dress skirted past her, slashing her attacker's leg and trying in vain to stab him.

"Olivia!" shouted Remei. "Get back inside!"

"We stand with you," said Olivia, her sword arm shaking as she struggled to hold it steady. Behind her a crowd of refugees poured out of the house, swords in hand ready to fight.

"Retreat! Regroup!" shouted the militia leader, seeing his followers being dropped steadily by Nestor's experienced and furious hand, backed up by the refugees his arrival had rallied.

"Cowards!" shouted Nestor, as Kai'til's men sprinted back down the hill away from the refuge. "After them!"

The refugees whooped and began to flow out of the building in pursuit.

"No, stop!" screamed Remei. "*Stop!*"

Nestor raised his hand and signaled everyone to obey. "What is it, Remei?"

"You will not hunt them down," she said emphatically. "Blood for blood will solve nothing here."

"They killed my sister!" a man protested.

"They cut off my father's ear!" another said.

"Enough!" she said, silencing their complaints. "They have committed atrocities far more *okal'a'ni* than anything we would have ever imagined. But it is their souls which are tainted now— don't ruin yours by mimicking them." *As I have*, she thought bleakly. She didn't know what firing the gun meant. All she knew, for sure, was that the moment she feared for Nestor's life, she had to do it.

There were several cries of protest, and Nestor had to fight the urge to give into his desire for bloodshed. "Sh— she's right," he said, clenching his teeth and sheathing his sword. "While we have a sense of morality, we can still win the cause. If we sink to their level, they've already won."

It took some shouts and arguments, but Nestor and Remei managed to calm the refugees down. They started filing back toward the house with the promise of a plan ahead.

"Voltan!" shouted Olivia, looking from face to face and child to child in an attempt to find her brother as she pushed past the slow-moving and tired fighters. "Voltan!"

"Where have you been?" Remei said, a mixture of worry and anger on her face as she looked at Nestor.

"I've been fighting and running from Kai'til's men."

"The children needed you," she said, standing outside with him as the refugees filed back into the house. The gun hung in her hand. Fixed to it as if by glue. And yet half-forgotten. "I needed you."

"I'm sorry," said Nestor. He stared down at the gun she was holding as if he wondered whether she might raise it and fire at him. "I came as soon as I saw them heading up the hill."

"We could have been killed," snapped Remei, then her face turned ghostly white. "Where's Enid?"

Without a word, they dashed into the house, pushing past people as they scoured the rooms, eventually ending up in Enid's room. The window was open and muddy foot-prints marked the roof and the floor where someone had entered.

"No," said Remei, moaning. "No, it can't be."

"Gods," whispered Nestor, taking in quick, sharp breaths.

"You promised me you'd protect us!" snapped Remei in anguish, tears flowing down her cheeks as she rounded on Nestor. "You said you'd keep us safe!" She pounded on his chest hysterically. The gun in her hand still.

"I tried," Nestor said, the pressure in his chest feeling as though his heart would burst. "I can't be everywhere at once." He wrenched the gun away from her. "Where did you get this?" he asked her.

Remei ignored the question. "Be there for your family!" she said, blubbering. Her eyes narrowed and she threw up her arms. "Not for the liege of some house to which we don't even belong."

"We don't belong anywhere," snapped Nestor, leaning in as his face heated. "And so we might as well be here as be anywhere else. This isn't Di Mon's fault. You're the one harboring the fugitives as though they're your own."

Her eyes widened in fury. "Oh, so it's my fault now? I should have turned these 'fugitives' away, should I?"

"Maybe Enid wouldn't be gone if you weren't so eager to help the refugees, yes," Nestor said testily, then immediately regretted it.

Remei's jaw dropped and she slapped Nestor hard across the face. "You find my son," she said, "or go be a fugitive yourself." Without another word she stormed from the room and slammed the door, making one of Enid's toys fall from its shelves and land with a loud *crack* on the floor.

"Fine!" Nestor shouted. He was about to follow her out when the sight of the toy stopped him. Their Enid was gone. Again. And like Remei said, it was his fault.

He stooped down and cradled the toy in his hands, before his chest heaved and he started sobbing.

Chapter 9

Voltan crashed through the fields of Monitum as though he were a leaf falling through tangled branches. When he had made it far enough away and down the hill, he stopped to take in his surroundings, and his visual perceptions shifted the color and hue of everything around him. The impact of his feet on the ground sent shudders up through his skull, which he hoped would throw a stick into the gears of his racing mind.

In the distance he could see the spaceport his father had once administered, dozens of soldiers patrolling the perimeter defined by an encircling fence. Voltan wondered if the soldiers had found the small gaps and weak link sections that he, Pleo and Olivia once used to sneak in and out of the compound. The pattern of the guards' patrols drew themselves out rapidly in Voltan's mind and, blinking his eyes several times as the puzzle came together, he made a move toward one of the gaps in the security.

He lay in the grass with a stick in hand as a guard marched by him, and he found himself unafraid. His mental assessment of the situation gave him a confidence that he had never before felt. Even when he thought of the dangers of his hubris he couldn't see errors in his assessment or bring himself to doubt.

The guard passed and Voltan slid under the fence, bending it over top of him as he pulled himself along the ground on his back. Shimmying the rest of the way, he rolled over to see the nearby ventilation fans that stood half a story tall and blew a steady stream of hot air over his skin. He got up and sprinted to the fan, the familiar heat making his skin prickle until he got close enough to smell the rusting spaceport's bowels. Holding his stick against the fan gradually slowed its revolutions, making a loud *rat-tat-tat*. He took a deep breath the blades turned. Shouts sounded behind him. With a twitch of hesitation, he waited for another few rotations then leapt through the gap, protecting his body from the sharp front edge with the stick as he spun through and landed on the other side.

He was sweating so much now that his shirt was starting to steam. With practiced motions, he spat on his hands as he opened one of the hot access panels. There were two exposed wires that he shorted to divert the flow of hot air elsewhere, keeping the fan going but making the system think the exhaust vent was out of commission. The wires sparked as he brought them together. He used his shirt to twist them.

Panting, with eyes wide and his vision still swimming in different colors, he waited for the temperature to drop. The guards grunted at one another on the other side of the fan, looking at it suspiciously. It was spinning at full speed now, and the thought that anyone or anything could have gotten through must have never crossed their minds. It had occurred to Voltan only because he knew everything there was to know about the mechanics of the system.

Smiling, Voltan wiped his forehead with his sleeve and started moving through the ventilations ducts. The lingering air rippled around him as he wove through the maze, the familiar twists and turns slowing his pulse and easing the torrent of mental flow. The ducts narrowed and eventually he was crawling, the metal occasionally ringing when his shoe rubbed it the wrong way.

He came to an opening and peered out at a small room where two men whispered together.

"Hurry, before someone finds us," said one, a black-haired man of the Monatese guard.

"Amazing that all this time the key was in here!" said the other man, holding up a syringe loaded with a slightly purple, transparent liquid.

"Yes, wonderful, let's get it over with." The black-haired man rolled up his sleeve to expose his veined arm.

Voltan closed his eyes when the liquid was injected, and kept crawling.

"What if they find out?" Voltan heard the man say with a tremor of uncertainty.

"Are you kidding? They'll only find out through your children, if ever, and by that time this whole thing will have been forgotten."

We'll have been forgotten, thought Voltan, frowning.

He reached a side panel in the duct and pried it open, eventually kicking it because it was slightly jammed. The panel fell to reveal a small, dirty alcove filled with knick-knacks with a pile of pillows in one corner. Crumbs and debris covered the ground and Voltan stooped down to squash a chunk of dry bread with his hand. As the powdered remains slid between the cracks of his fingers, he smiled. *I'm back.*

He picked up a sphere with a thin disk protruding from its equator. The insides were transparent, marked with a series of interconnecting paths forming an intricate maze. Voltan picked it up delicately, running his hands across the smooth surface. In the center he could see a trapped marble that rolled around as he tilted the sphere. He took a seat atop the throne of pillows, and began tilting the sphere this way and that, relishing the focus provided by his favorite puzzle.

In a few minutes the marble tumbled out and he watched it bounce across the hard floor in sharp snaps before a crumb ended its series of parabolic leaps. He fetched the marble and, turning the disk in a grinding movement inside the sphere, began to weave the marble back to the center via a different path.

The puzzle proved easier than he remembered, and soon he was getting bored, his vision shimmering with color as his mind went into overdrive, analyzing and assessing every detail.

With a shout, he threw the puzzle across the room. It struck the floor with a thud of plastic. Voltan got up and paced around the room a few minutes before he got back into the tunnel, clutching the sides of his head in an effort to stop the noise.

Voltan crawled through the tunnel and stopped above a large study. His skin bristled, and he closed his eyes to visualize the map of the spaceport. This room wasn't supposed be here. He leaned and peered through the cracks to make sure no one was nearby before he pried off the ventilation grate.

The stacks of books inside reminded him of his father's office, outside, but as far as Voltan knew, this area of the spaceport was supposed to be filled with control systems hardware, with a separate ventilation system. He walked around and scanned the titles, which included some Old Earth stories that he had thought were simply made up by his father. The titles jumped out at him and he tried to turn away to focus on the well-worn chair or the picture frames depicting mountain ranges and waterfalls. His gaze kept returning to the bookshelf, however, where he noticed several books that were out of alphabetical order.

One was entitled *The Fall* by Albert Camus. Another was *A Special Providence* by Richard Yates. There was *Grimm's Fairy Tales* by the Brothers Grimm, *Of Mice and Men* by John Steinbeck, *Frankenstein* by Mary Shelley, *Moby Dick* by Herman Melville and several other books that were in the wrong places. Instinctively, Voltan reached for *Moby Dick*, intending to correct the mis-shelving. When he pulled it, however, the book only tilted and came out halfway—something was holding it in. He tried the other books and the same thing happened for most of them.

Frowning, his eyes flitted over the titles. *It's a puzzle,* he thought. If the books needed to be tugged in a certain order, he quickly calculated that there were almost half a billion different combinations. It was impossible for him to try them all.

He tugged on *Grimm's Fairy Tales* and was surprised when the book came out. Flipping through it, he saw the "Little Red-Cap" story, "The Frog Prince" and "Hansel and Gretel". There was a crease in the pages at "The Dog and the Sparrow," on which he saw a massive picture of a sparrow. Reading the story left him more puzzled than ever. The story was about the friendship between a dog and a sparrow where the sparrow avenges the murder of the dog.

Voltan tried all the other books, and none of them budged. With eleven books, there were only forty million combinations, but that was still too much. His mind raced over the titles, trying to figure some meaning from them. *The Fall of mice and men,* he thought, thinking up ways to combine the titles and pulling the books in that order. *Moby Dick's special providence.*

He lost track of time as he stood before the dark bookcase, pulling on books until his arms were tired. Finally, he collapsed into a cross-legged seat on the carpet. That was when he remembered something. *There is special providence in the fall of a sparrow,* he thought, uncertain where he had read the aphorism. He stared dumbly at the bookshelf, wondering if he should try that combination. He would have to put *Grimm's Fairy Tales* back where he had found it, which seemed an odd mechanism to include in the lock. Pulling himself up, he tugged on *A Special Providence, The Fall* then placed *Grimm's Fairy Tales* back in its spot.

There was a low rumble and grinding of gears as the bookcase vibrated before it pushed out toward Voltan. He jumped back, afraid the shelves were about to topple over on top of him. When the rumbling stopped, he looked around the bookshelf and saw that there was a small opening in its side, and the entire thing had pivoted as though it were a door. His heart pounded as he tried to imagine where the passage fit into the building's layout. He'd studied the blueprints as soon as he'd been old enough to understand them, and they contained nothing of the details staring him in the face. Swallowing hard, he slid into the dark passage beyond.

Olivia's muscles ached, an after-effect of the spasms of a clear dream. It took an effort of will to remain standing with Remei in her bedroom. Normally, the sight of the flowered tapestries and balanced space would have soothed her, but now it just seemed to make her head hurt.

"I have to find the boys," Remei said, her brow creased with lines.

"I'll help you," Olivia replied.

"No, you must take care of the refugees." Remei looked down at the floor as though she could see through it to the hordes below. "They need someone strong to guide them."

I'm not, thought Olivia. *I couldn't take care of my own family. What makes you think I can take care of these people?* "There must be someone else," she said.

"Olivia, you fought when the need arose," Remei said, putting her hands on Olivia's shoulders. "There is no one better."

"I wish I had your confidence."

Remei's expression turned solemn and her exhaustion showed. "No, you don't."

Olivia watched as Nestor and Remei silently packed their bags and readied to head into the heart of the capitol. Several of the refugees protested their departure. Some offered to go with them but Nestor refused, insisting that they needed to travel stealthily and wouldn't risk the lives of the refugees. Many felt like they were being abandoned by Remei, and it was only at the end that they dared cry out against their exhausted host.

"You're leaving us to die!"

"You've given up!"

Nestor looked disgusted as he turned around, his lips pursed in an angry expression that he maintained as the shouts continued and the clamor rose. "Enough!" he shouted when he could stand no more, his voice a roar above the cacophony of protests. "We have not given up, but it sounds like you have."

Curses and shouts answered him as several people advanced, and he stepped forward to meet them. "You think Remei's responsible for protecting you? You think I am? If you depend on one man or woman for salvation, abandoning all hope otherwise, what does that say about your strength? Your resolve, your willingness to fight to survive?" He scanned the crowd as they fell silent. "You speak of strength as though someone can serve it to you for dinner. You speak of determination as though there is someone else who can do it for you." His jaw relaxed after a moment, and he went on more softly. "Each of you has already demonstrated that you're willing to fight, run and work together in order to survive. Just open your eyes and see it."

Olivia thought that Nestor looked like he hadn't been sleeping any more than Remei. She pushed through to the front of the crowd and nodded at Nestor before turning to speak. She swallowed. "I will take you to safety," Olivia said, "but I will need your help."

"You're just a child!" someone protested.

"What do you know of struggle or survival?" another said.

Something snapped within Olivia, and her face curled in anger. "What do I know of struggle?" she yelled, shoving the man who had uttered it and knocking him to the ground. "I watched my parents get murdered and made it out alive. I've been running and searching for my brother, going back into the belly of *okal'a'ni* evil almost every night. Whoever else dares to trivialize my experience by my age, I challenge to step forward now, and we will see whose blade is sharper." She reached over and quickly grabbed Nestor's sword, startling him. She slid it out of its sheath before he could stop her and held it toward the crowd, silently hoping no one would take her up on the challenge, but at the same time relishing an opportunity to let loose her frustration.

The silence stretched until a child came forward, squirming away from his parents. "Where are we going to go?" he asked.

Olivia stared at the wide-eyed boy, his clothes marked with mud stains that wouldn't wash out. "South," she said, trying to maintain the illusion of certainty. "There are hiding places Kai'til doesn't know about. And we just have hold out until order is restored." She didn't mention her doubts about whether it ever would be.

Nestor touched her shoulder. "How will we contact you?"

She flipped the sword up and gripped the blade lightly, extending the handle toward him. "How did you find us the first time?"

"I was lucky," he whispered. "We can't rely on that again."

"We have to," Olivia replied. "Kai'til has control of official communications and he might be monitoring for independent signals. As you said, we'll be okay on our own.

Besides, you have to worry about yourselves. Find Enid. And find my brothers."

Nestor held her gaze for several seconds before finally grabbing his sword. "I give you my word, Lady Ald'erda."

"I don't want anything except my family," she said, her expression serious. "Voltan was always fond of speaking through action. Honor him by doing the same."

Nestor bowed, closing his eyes. Remei came forward to hug Olivia, eyes wet with tears. "Take care, my child. You are strong and beautiful."

Olivia resisted the urge to melt into the embrace, and whispered back, "At least you fell for it."

Remei pulled away and winked at her, before turning and walking down the hill. She and Nestor didn't say a word to one another, and Olivia wondered how long they would stay mad before remembering they loved each other.

A hand touched her shoulder softly, and she turned to see Faren's face beaming at her. "What next, m'Lady?"

She scanned the crowd. "Let's pack what we can from the house. We set out in an hour."

Chapter 10

Voltan ran his hand across the rough, cold metal as everything went black. The ground sloped steadily downward as he wove in and around the thick supports of the spaceport. He felt a strange sense of satisfaction at having uncovered a mystery that, had he not grown up reading as much as he did, he would never have figured out. He wondered if he was going to find a buried chest full of so much money that he could pay everyone to stop fighting. Or maybe there was something that would bring his parents back.

The ground flattened and began rising. It was surprisingly hot and sticky now, and Voltan found himself rubbing sweat from his brow every few minutes as the passage led on. He had flitting doubts about possible danger at the end of the tunnel, but kept suppressing them by calculating that the likelihood of meeting the owner here *right now* was pretty low.

A dim light began to appear at the edge of sight: a gray, indiscriminate blur that he couldn't resolve no matter how hard he squinted. The brightness increased steadily and he had to stop to let his weary eyes adjust. He eventually saw a horizontal slit of light at the bottom of the passage as he rounded a corner.

Moving more carefully, he approached and found a wall that he would have thought was a dead end if not for the light penetrating beneath it. He lowered himself to the ground and tried to peer through the slit, but couldn't see anything. He nearly slipped when he tried to push himself up with sweaty hands, and breathed heavily as he sat on his knees and closed his eyes. *You can do this,* he thought, flexing and relaxing his muscles before standing. He pushed the wall with his shoulder and leaned, but nothing happened.

He pushed harder until he was ramming the wall with his full body weight. Voltan gave a shout as the door finally fell back into a blinding sea of light. *Was this what Mom and Dad saw?* he wondered.

Someone inhaled sharply and Voltan shrank back, extending his arms in a futile attempt to gain grounding. He trembled as he realized how helpless he was: a blind, lonely child deep underground.

"My, my," said a breathy man's voice, a hint of irritation in it. After a pause, the man continued in a warmer tone, "Well, hello there."

Voltan gulped. "Hi," he said.

"How did you manage to find your way down here, boy?"

"I... well— I like to solve puzzles and there was a book-shelf with all these books out of order, and I tried different combinations." The words poured out faster than Voltan had thought possible for himself. He wasn't sure how much of a chance the man would give him to explain. "Finally I tried a combination based on 'There is special providence in the fall of a sparrow' and followed the passage here."

The man laughed and Voltan could make out a tall, thin form in the light. "How on Monitum did you know that quote?"

"I don't know." Voltan frowned. "I read a lot, and must have seen it somewhere."

"Shakespeare," said the man, coming into sharper focus as Voltan's eyes relaxed into the light. He was skinny with wiry muscles pulled tight against his bones, and he was shirtless. A flattened sheath of receded black hair came into a V-shaped widow's peak high on his forehead. Around him bright-colored splotches covered the walls, except for one which had a giant painted map of the Empire's reaches. There was a bed with a small cage beside it, and Voltan squinted to see what was inside it.

"Have you heard of William Shakespeare, boy?" There was an expression of playful amusement on the man's face.

"M— maybe," Voltan said, trembling.

"Brilliant Old Earth writer," said the man. "The average Gelack would probably confuse him with a Lorel." A wheezy laugh. "Most of Monitum wouldn't have a clue, either. Which makes you quite special."

Voltan nodded. "Thank you, sir."

"You needn't call me sir. We are equals, you and I, as you clearly demonstrated by coming all the way down here. I am Prokhor Lor'Vrel." He gave a slight bow, bending one arm behind his back.

Lor'Vrel? thought Voltan. *Aren't they nearly gone or extinct?* He caught Prokhor looking at him expectantly, and stuttered, "I am Voltan… Ald'erda." It was the first time he had said his family name since someone else had uttered the words and condemned his father.

Prokhor nodded slowly, a smile twitching at the corners of his lips before softening into an expression of sympathy. "You've been through a lot, young man, haven't you?"

Voltan stared at him, then nodded.

"There is so much hatred boiling within the Vrellish," Prokhor went on. "They're like animals, and as soon as a chance presents itself, they will pounce." He paused, furrowing his brow slightly as he looked sideways at Voltan. "Tell me, Voltan, why did you notice the books were out of order?"

Voltan shifted from one foot to another. "I… my mind won't shut off. It's constantly going, and it's getting worse." He couldn't keep the pain from his voice.

Prokhor nodded knowingly. "You know, I have the exact same problem," he said. "You know who is known for having such a common problem?"

Voltan shook his head.

"Lorels," said Prokhor.

Voltan's face sank into a frown. "Great," he said. "Everyone hates Lorels."

"Not everyone," Prokhor said, lifting a finger. "In fact, in almost every other regard Lorels are indistinguishable from other Sevolites."

"It doesn't matter," Voltan replied. "People will find a reason to hate you no matter what." He paused, pursing his lips. "And I'm not a Lorel."

"Of course you're not," Prokhor said soothingly. "But you seem to possess some of the finest qualities of one. And no matter what anyone says, Voltan, you must never be ashamed of who you are."

Voltan stared at the strange Lor'Vrel and wondered once more if his father's spirit had been reborn in another man. "Why am I like this?"

"It might be a side-effect of what your father did to his blood," Prokhor suggested. "I think it is a gift that is worth developing, Voltan. I can help you, if you like, to learn ways to calm the infernal machine of your mind and use it to better ends."

Is this what you meant for me, Dad? Voltan thought. *Is this fight a puzzle that remains to be solved?*

Burnt ground stretched out before Remei and Nestor, the smell of ashes and smoke a reminder of the permanent damage done.

"What happened to *Okal Rel*?" whispered Remei.

Nestor stooped beside her to run charcoal through his fingertips. The breakdown of *Okal Rel* had happened in the Nesak war, here and there, but it had never been as bad as this. Even Remei had been driven to use a gun. His heart felt heavy as he stared out over the senseless waste. The ground would heal in time, but the environmental damage was as close to the definition of *okal'a'ni* as you could get. He was torn between rage and hilarity at the thought of the hunters committing worse atrocities than those they hunted, and doing it in a way so blatant it could go into a Nesak textbook for alarming children.

He closed his eyes and stood, knees straightening with a weary tightness that made him wonder if he could start wearing out from the inside, even if he couldn't get old in the usual way of commoners. He shot a glance at Remei, who continued to avoid eye contact. His eyelids drooped. He scanned the horizon for their next path, then beckoned Remei to move on.

They skirted another barren-looking village, and Nestor was thankful that at least this one wasn't burnt to the ground. Convinced they could enter without being noticed, they stalked between buildings too silent for the lifestyle they had been constructed to support.

Walking across the deck of a pub, Nestor froze and plastered himself to the ruined wall. "Do you hear that?" he whispered.

Remei had followed his example, and her wide eyes darted around. She nodded. Whispers came from inside the pub. She made a motion with her head for them to flee, but Nestor frowned.

"Survivors," he mouthed.

Remei glared at him, but nevertheless he peered around the doorframe of the bar. Convinced no one was in sight, he crept in, keeping himself below table height as he avoided broken glass in and around the seats.

An island in the middle divided the bar in two. Nestor crept to the back, his hand on his hilt. When he got into the second half of the room, he smelt death and decay. Bile rose in his throat at the sight of corpses scattered around, some with sword-in-hand. *At least these ones had a chance to fight,* he thought, and searched for the source of the noise.

A man with a gaping mouth leaned against a table, his eyes filled with a mound of insects that twitched and bulged as Nestor approached. He covered his mouth, and realized that the sound wasn't a whisper at all. It was coming from a piece of nervecloth dangling off the man's ear.

Reaching a hand out, Nestor peeled off the nervecloth. A small, flesh-colored speaker came with it. He could make out a few of the muffled words of a man's voice just by holding it near his head.

"We take the opportunity to thank the brave Grianach army for their prompt actions in taking responsibility for protecting the peace under *Okal Rel* in their region. To those soldiers listening, all of Monitum owes you a debt of gratitude for the steps you are now taking to ensure that the current, corrupt institutions can be made pure for our children.

"The menace of self-interested, illegal bioengineering of offspring was brought to light through the actions of Liege Ald'erda, erstwhile Sheriff of Grianach who should have been concerned to uphold the very laws he violated. Correcting the mess has presented great challenges that we have fought through valiantly and with honor. Please remember to take time to gather your energy, and avoid whatever can divide you and disperse your strength. You must be strong because you are at war with Lorel evil, now, as surely as our ancestors in the Purification Wars of long ago. And like them, we, too, can prevail."

Nestor felt dizzy as he saw flecks of black creep into his vision. Swallowing hard, he shivered as he raised his shoulders and shrank down to try to hide the sick feeling in his stomach. He held the nervecloth away from himself as though it could infect him.

"Nestor!" called Remei in a loud whisper from the front. "Please come out," she added in a whimper.

Looking at the man whose eyes had been eaten out, Nestor thought, *Your mind was gone well before the insects got here.* He stood up slowly, letting his free arm flop loosely at his side as the man on the speaker continued to chatter on and congratulate the brave soldiers of the Grianach Purification War.

A wave of relief passed over Remei's face as she saw him come out, then she looked away and crossed her arms impatiently.

"Remei," said Nestor slowly, as he walked toward her, his limbs feeling weak. "You have to hear this."

Her frown deepened as he approached and brought the speaker to her ear.

"Sheriff Kai'til has held a meeting in which you, the citizens, have spoken, and your voices have been heard. The power of the people has led to the following conclusions in order for a smooth transition to a just and prosperous society.

"The population has to respect each other and live in peace in this time of crisis. No one should challenge another. We need solidarity, brothers and sisters.

"Everyone has a responsibility to help one another and fight against the *okal'a'ni* traitors who threaten to rob Monitum of its blood heritage through abominations of Lorel science. Together, we must fight as one.

"We must be united and identify the enemy, who may be right next to you. They are *not* your friends and neighbors. They are the reason for this tragedy. They are the reason for the struggle. The gate to the future can only open once they are removed from the path.

"Sheriff Kai'til will give a formal statement in an hour, so keep your nervecloth active, brothers and sisters. For now, this is Paxasa, signing off."

The sound of woodwinds came on, playing a famous piece by Hyssop of Sanctuary, a Monatese musician from the era of the Purification Wars. It was said to speak in the voice of Old Earth and paint a picture of a green land rich with potential and beauty. Nestor had heard it before, and in any other circumstance he would have enjoyed listening to it.

"How many people were wearing one of these?" Remei breathed, incredulous.

"It's impossible to say," Nestor said, holding the earpiece at eye level. "It blends in with the skin and the speaker is covered. Anyone could have it. Gods know how long people have had them. But I suspect Kai'til was organizing behind Ald'erda's back long before he exposed him, playing the devoted deputy."

Remei's face twisted in pain and her lips trembled. Tears formed at the corners of her eyes and she started breathing heavily. "Why?" she murmured. "Who would do this?"

Nestor tentatively touched her shoulder, and she sank toward him. He wrapped his arms around her, grateful for the warm feeling of her cheek against his neck and her body pressed against his. "I don't know," he whispered.

His wife sobbed softly into his shoulder, causing tears to stream down his own cheeks. He held his thumb over the speaker of the nervecloth so they wouldn't have to listen to it. They stood together for a while like this, in the ruined and stench-filled bar as the shadows lengthened outside.

"It was more manageable when I thought it was hysteria," said Remei. "When people were lashing out, in the heat of the moment. A mob."

Nestor closed his eyes and slightly nodded his head against hers. "I know," he said. "I know."

Chapter 11

Pleo's heart raced as the man fell to the ground, his face dripping blood and his hands tied behind his back. There was a clear sense of righteousness in the moment, and Pleo wanted more than anything to finish the traitor off himself. Resisting the urge, he took a few steps back, letting the baton fall to his side as he turned to face the seven children in the dim alley who watched in either fear or awe. Pleo needed to ensure that the emotion was the latter.

"Enid," he commanded, looking at the quaking youth with the strange lizard perched on his shoulder. "This is your chance to serve justice today." He extended the baton as an offering, although his body language made it clear it wasn't much of a choice.

Enid's lips trembled as he stood still. "N— no," he said. "I won't."

Pleo's face curled into a sneer. "Are you saying you'd rather let this man walk free? That you'd be content to sit back and watch while your friends and family are murdered?" With each phrase he took a heavy step toward Enid.

The lizard growled as Pleo approached, and Enid shrank into his hunched shoulders.

"If you won't strike, it makes you this man's friend," said Pleo, looking over his shoulder at the bloody, gasping man. "And what is the friend of our enemy?" He scanned the group of boys.

"An enemy!" cried one of the smaller boys, excited that he could understand this concept better than Pleo's other words.

"Do we let our enemies walk free?" Pleo went on.

"No!" shouted the boys together, and they began kicking the man on the ground. All except Enid.

"Stop!" shouted Pleo, but it took them a few moments to disengage from their frenzy. When he had shoved them apart, he looked down at the man. He no longer moved. "He was to be Enid's kill today!" Pleo yelled. His temper cooled as he took in the fury in the boys' eyes that told him they would resist the amount of control he wanted to place on them. He had to keep a careful balance between letting them loose and tightening the leash. "You all carried out justice, though, so today is still a good day," he concluded.

The boys whooped and cheered as they went back to kicking the dead man. Three of the boys dragged Enid over and pushed him into the center of the circle, right next to the dead man.

"Come on, Enid!" shouted Sigurd.

"He's already dead," another boy encouraged him.

"You can't hurt a dead guy."

Enid breathed in short, panicked breaths as his head turned from side to side looking for a way out. The boys' feral cries terrified him, and he had no doubt that they would turn on him if he didn't act soon. The man was already dead, after all. *I'm sorry,* he thought, as he gave the body a swift kick to the chest.

The boys whooped, urging him to do it again. He repeated the act until the boys lifted him up on their shoulders, bobbing up and down triumphantly. In an instant the feelings around him had gone from hostility to warm embrace, and the security was a great comfort. He couldn't help but smile a little as they started chanting his name.

"Have you ever seen a protein, Voltan?" Prokhor asked, smiling at the wide-eyed boy who walked beside him in the pristine, white environment of a laboratory. He realized he was getting ahead of himself. "Beautiful, isn't it?"

Voltan nodded, barely paying attention to Prokhor as his mind scanned the instruments, visually dissecting them and discerning their function based on their structures. Prokhor began to explain the various centrifuges, fridges, scanners and diagnostics that had nervecloth wiring running in a mess everywhere. Anyone else would have probably thought the room was a disaster, but Voltan could see the potential of everything — like a tool belt that could be used to penetrate nature's most puzzling secrets.

"Here, you'll like this," said Prokhor, lifting a hood toward Voltan.

"What is it?" Voltan asked, leaning left and right to try and see a clue as to the hood's function.

"A protein visualizer. It lets you see and manipulate models of proteins, so that you can understand how to unfold certain structures." Prokhor held up a pair of gloves with sensory tips that must have been for the manipulation and folding that he had mentioned.

"Why do you want to fold them?" Voltan asked.

"Proteins are the most important molecules in our bodies," Prokhor explained. "Named after an ancient word, *protos*, meaning primary. They are made up of only twenty different building blocks, but the way they form chains and fold together is very difficult to determine, or emulate."

Voltan frowned as he took in the information. "So you try different structures to see if they perform the function you expect?"

"Kind of," Prokhor said. "We can figure out the number of building blocks easily, but it's not easy to figure out how to build them to get the right results."

Voltan put on the hood, and instantly a complicated set of loops and twists appeared before him. Sliding his hands into the gloves Prokhor offered him, Voltan let out a "Wow," as he began turning the model and searching its nooks and crannies. There was so much to look at, so much to explore, that the mental chatter in his head quieted, and for several minutes he forgot where they were.

When he had unfolded the protein, he took the hood off and let out a heavy sigh of relief. "That felt good," he said, sighing again.

Prokhor smiled at him. "That's the best way I've found to quiet my mind," he said. "Immerse myself totally in whatever I'm doing. But in order for me to do that, the project has to be challenging enough. Thankfully," he gestured at his surroundings, "there are a considerable number of complex puzzles that remain to be solved here. And I could very much use your help, Voltan."

Voltan blinked and thought of how many problems had been totally out of reach— his parents, his sister, his brother. The protein problems were something he could wrap his mind around and get a handle on. And if proteins were as useful as Prokhor said, he might be able to do something, indirectly, about everything else.

In the streets leading up to the spaceport, Nestor and Remei crouched in the darkness behind a restaurant's trash bin. Nestor had the talking nervecloth plastered to his ear, listening to the stream of distortions as though they might yield a clue to penetrating the dense web of guards around the spaceport. It was infuriating to have made it this far, and be blocked by Di Mon's own troops— who had arrived, at last, but were working for Kai'til. They were listening to the same stream as him, and now that he knew of its existence, he could see the men adjusting the nervecloth on the sides of their heads quite often. Some of them frowned uncertainly, but far too few for comfort. Most of them were lapping it up just like the locals.

"The blight on our society stems from those who act out of purely selfish motives for their own personal gain, instead of that of the nation. They think nothing of the greater whole, of the larger picture on which they and their families have depended for centuries. They would have *Okal Rel* abolished. They have already demonstrated this by burning our beautiful green land.

"Some of these abominations would have you think that they want nothing but peaceful coexistence. Do not fall for these lies. They will only exist peacefully until their children have grown up and can press for segregation for the lower classes, the very same stock from which the *okal'a'ni* abominations come. They will subjugate those, like you, who stand on the moral apex for not succumbing to the Lorel temptation. Those, like you, who accept their place in the natural order, and wait for *honest* opportunities to better themselves through children in future lives."

Nestor and Remei crouched lower as they watched the same guard pass by who, among others, had been circling for hours. They couldn't find a gap to go through, and it looked like they would be waiting a while unless they risked blatant exposure. They couldn't even to go back the way they had come in.

Remei was tired, bags under her eyes and her skin pale and bluish. She sat with her back against the wall behind the trash, staring off into the distance. A few hours ago they had been troubled by the stench of the garbage. Now they could smell nothing at all.

"The children needed you," she whispered, still staring at nothing. "Especially Voltan."

Nestor's jaw tightened in anger, and he had to fight to keep his voice down. "I'm sorry," he said. "If I made the wrong choice, there's nothing I can do to change it."

Remei looked away from him.

"What do you want me to say?" he murmured. "That I will lash myself every day for the next ten years for my oversight? Would you have honestly done any differently?"

"I did do differently," snapped Remei, her words harsh and crisp. "I was there for my family."

"You were distracted by the refugees," Nestor said, feeling sick with the sense of *deja vu* as well as the realization that he couldn't back down.

"At least I was within earshot of the children." Remei lifted her head to peer over the trash bins. "Maybe I should call your pal Di Mon— he's bound to take our side and come running just as you did for him, right?"

Nestor's face darkened, and he pursed his lips, saying nothing. The nervecloth chattered away in his ear. "The *okal'a'ni* want to teach you to flee, and to be afraid. We have stood up and said that we will not learn that lesson."

Nestor sighed, depressed by the incessant ugliness around him. How many times would he and Remei have this argument? It seemed like every time things started looking grim, the same animosity came out between them.

"We will find Enid, and Voltan, too," he said quietly, scratching the ground between his feet to have something to focus on.

"How can you promise that?" Remei asked, her brow furrowed.

"Because I know that I won't stop looking. And if that's not good enough for you, Remei, I don't know what will be."

Remei stayed silent, looking down as she chewed on her lip.

"Some people have asked whether or not Liege Monitum supports our cause," said the voice in Nestor's nervecloth. "To those people, I ask this: would he have deployed as many troops from outside the province if he didn't? He has delegated this work to Sheriff Kai'til. Be satisfied that he is with us, and that he has granted us the resources to do the job."

Nestor twitched and shook in an effort to get rid of a chill that rose through his spine. "Maybe you're right," he muttered to Remei. "Maybe we should just call out for him."

"What are you talking about?" asked Remei. "How? Kai'til controls communications."

"Di Mon hasn't left the planet yet to return to court. We have to get through before he does. If he sees anyone trying to stop us, he'll know what's really going on," Nestor explained. "If we can move fast enough, then we can get within sight of his guard before Kai'til's men can catch us."

"You're forgetting that they're not afraid to use firearms," said Remei, a queasy look crossing her face.

Nestor bit his lip. "All right. You can stay here. I'm going to risk it."

"Like purgatory you are," Remei said, looking him up and down. "I just thought it was worth mentioning, you know, so we can prepare ourselves to be riddled with *okal'a'ni'* holes."

"Kai'til would say the holes are vessels through which our evil toxins can be expunged."

"I'll make sure to return the courtesy if we see him," she growled.

The stores on either side of the street rose to about half the height of the looming spaceport which seemed close enough to touch, but was farther away than it looked. Only its size made it look so close. The walls of the streets were caked with grime, a stark contrast to the sleek and shiny form of Laedan's spaceport. Nestor wondered if the maintenance of the port had superseded other societal needs during Laedan's rule, and if that, in part, had been why so many people easily turned against him. Maybe Laedan Ald'erda was partly to blame for the contempt he'd felt towards those less ambitious than himself. The contempt that had been mirrored back, amplified. Nothing was ever simple. However, it was crystal clear to Nestor no child born altered by a parent's greed was guilty of anything.

Nestor grabbed a bag of garbage, cracked it open and began sifting through it. Weighing several wet pieces of metal in his hands, a disgusted look crossed his face before he seemed satisfied.

"What are you doing?" asked Remei.

"Getting tools for distraction."

Remei reluctantly grabbed a few of the pieces herself.

"Ready?" Nestor asked. She nodded.

He launched a chunk of metal far down the street. It seemed to move in slow motion. The air whipped around it and the sun glinted off buildings as the piece spun around. It clattered to the ground.

The guard patrolling the street rushed down to see what was going on.

"Now!" ordered Nestor.

He and Remei darted out and into the adjoining street, to peer around the next corner. Another patrol was marching toward them, and so Nestor launched another chunk of metal over the building and farther down the street. When the metal clanged to the ground, the patrol turned around, giving Nestor and Remei enough time to cross.

The sky sparkled with the reflections off the shards that Nestor threw as he wove through the streets. He caught Remei smiling. They were only four blocks away from the spaceport.

"Fellow warriors," said the voice in Nestor's ear, "I've just received news that there are rebels on the verge of penetrating the spaceport. We cannot allow their filth to touch our great Liege Monitum. Nor can we allow their taint to risk spreading to other worlds. We must all accept responsibility for the well-being of Gelack and Monatese society, and stop them at all costs.

"A disturbance was reported to be somewhere between History Square and Philosopher's Alley. Concentrate all your efforts there, brethren, and may your Watching Dead bless your patriotic actions."

Gulping, Nestor watched the man he was about to distract turn around and run toward the corner behind which he and Remei perched. He heard a yell behind them and turned to see a soldier pointing a finger, who was quickly joined by several compatriots.

"Run." He grabbed Remei's hand, dropping most of the debris he had intended to use. He hurled metal at the soldier to their left, catching him in the forehead and knocking him down. The soldiers behind them shouted angrily, their voices raising war cries elsewhere.

The walls of the street seemed to close in around them as soldiers came in from side streets. Gunshots rang out as the bullets slapped the ground right beside them, inexpertly aimed. They had made it one block— three more to go.

Monatese fleet *sha* in occupation gear appeared in the streets ahead, and Remei slowed, panting. Tugging harder on her arm, Nestor kept running. "If we stop we die," he said, gasping for air. "We're plowing right through them."

The air seemed too quiet around Nestor as he approached a jeering mob of traditionally armed militia barring the road, swords held ready. When he was a few meters from them, he tossed a chunk of metal in the air, raising a few of their gazes for a precious second. He leapt forward with his sword and slit one man's throat, tearing the weapon out of his hands. The two nearest men lunged at him and he jumped back, deflecting their jabs with both of his swords.

He watched Remei approach him as he used his peripheral vision to parry his two attackers. Another soldier went for Remei and he cried out in fury, ducking and darting to one side, drawing one of his blades across a man's thigh. He kicked the other militia man and darted forward to stab Remei's attacker. The militia were amateurs compared with a Nersallian-trained warrior. But there were so many of them!

An instinctive, animal feeling prompted Nestor to dodge the instant before a blade grazed his side. He spun around, elbowing the soldier in the face with one arm as he continued turning to thrust his sword into his first opponent's eye. Kicking the dying enemy over, he dropped one sword and pulled Remei close to him, surging through the temporary gap they had made.

"Stop them!"

"Long live Kai'til!" Gunshots rang out in a scattering of excited shots as the men yelled.

The shots and cries were farther behind than their immediate pursuers, and Nestor didn't want to know how many soldiers were now amassed and squeezing them in. They were a block from the spaceport entrance now, where a few guards stood watching from the doors, looking astonished.

Nestor felt a sharp pain in his calf as a bullet tore into it. He cried out, staggering. Remei caught him before he fell, and helped him limp on.

"Di Mon!" screamed Nestor. "We are here to see Liege Monitum. You cannot bar us entry! He will have your heads!"

The men looked at one another, then back at Nestor and Remei. The two stopped a few meters away from the line, Nestor's hand shaking as his leg sent jets of pain up through his back.

"I am one of Di Mon's closest advisors. A friend," said Nestor, swallowing to try and wet his dry mouth. "You must let me speak with him. He alone will decide my fate, and whether or not I am a traitor."

"He is the one who harbored the fugitives!" one of the excited militia men accused Nestor.

"I challenge you to defy your Liege and strike me down," said Nestor, scanning the men but resting his gaze on his accuser. "You will experience a wrath unlike any you've ever tasted."

"Halt!" said the commander of the guards, raising his hand at the encroaching mob behind them.

Nestor resisted the urge to clutch to Remei, since it would make him appear weak.

"You were indeed a loyal retainer of Di Mon's," said the man in a booming voice. "Whether you still are remains to be judged. Silence!" he shouted at the cries of fury that rose up through the crowd. "He is right in one respect. Di Mon shall determine your fate. But since I suspect you are a spy for the traitors, you will be stripped of all possible weaponry."

Nestor tossed his sword down on the ground at the commander's feet.

Shouts and jeers sang out from the mob. "He could be concealing poisons! Strip him down!"

The commander's eyes narrowed as he weighed his options. By the power in his voice and the ease with which he worked with the crowd's desires, he had evidently had a lot of experience dealing with riots. "That is a possibility we cannot neglect," he admitted, nodding slowly. He motioned for the guards at his sides to move in.

"What happened to *Okal Rel*?" Nestor spat. "Sword Law? Honor?"

"Quiet," said the guard approaching Nestor. "If you have nothing to hide, you have nothing to fear." He reached his sword through the clasp of Nestor's vest, and in a swift upper motion that nearly caught Nestor in the chin, sliced the vest. The crowd whooped.

"I can remove it," Nestor said, growling. He pulled off his vest and shirt, exposing a bruised bare chest of rippling muscle, slicked in sweat. Some of the sword-bearing women in the crowd whistled, which sparked some loud arguments.

Another guard had moved in on Remei, and the angry men forgot all about the women's misstep in admiring Nestor.

"Surely you can afford her the dignity of privacy, commander," said Nestor, struggling as the guard sliced off his belt. From the hesitation on the commander's face, Nestor could tell the man agreed with him. "There is no need to do this in public."

"What do you have to hide!" a nameless voice cried from among the crowd.

"That Nesak priest-lover needs to feel the shame of public scorn!"

"Commander," said Remei as a guard sliced a strap of her bra and sleeve. "This is disgraceful. If we are truly armed, we would not hide a weapon, impractically, below all layers of our vestments." The guard shook her by the arm, and she cried out.

Nestor tore off his pants. "Satisfied?"

"I'll search him," said a female guard, licking her lips as she approached Nestor. She ran her hands up and around him, gripping him firmly. He felt himself harden, and she brought her face close to his. "You know, if you weren't a Lorel-sympathizer, you'd probably be good in bed," she whispered seductively.

"Stay away from him, you wretch!" shouted Remei, reeling in the arms of her captor.

The woman kept her hands on Nestor a few seconds longer, squeezing him a final time before letting go. "He's got nothing," she said as she turned around.

Nestor moved over to Remei, shoving the guard back as he tried to keep him away. He placed himself firmly behind Remei and the crowd, blocking as much as he could of their view. "Just cooperate, Remei," he murmured. "The sooner we can see Di Mon, the safer we'll be."

She looked at him with wet eyes, her lips turning down in misery as she pulled down her pants. A loud, ecstatic cry of triumph at her humiliation passed through the crowd as she exposed her bare white legs.

Soon she was in her underwear, and the guard beside her was all too quick to begin his search. Remei yelped as he squeezed her too hard and pinched her inappropriately. Nestor gritted his teeth and dug his nails into the palms of his hands. The crowd cheered the entire time.

"That's enough!" said the commander after an uncomfortable amount of time.

The guard reluctantly released Remei and blew her a kiss. "She's unarmed," he said, nodding at the commander.

"Take them in," the commander ordered his guards. When the crowd motioned to follow, he snapped. "We can handle it from here! Get back to your posts and protect the city from encroachment. This is not a theatre! Back to work!"

There were many shouts of protest and men who spat on the ground in objection, but the crowd started to disperse.

The guards pushed Nestor and Remei inside roughly, shivers lancing up through their bare feet as they walked on the cold floor of the spaceport's entrance lobby.

"We should just kill them," suggested a guard as they walked on. The same one who had volunteered to search Remei.

"Enough!" snapped the commander. "It's bad enough those soldiers out there were being animals. I don't need my own warriors doing the same."

That silenced them, and Nestor closed his eyes for a moment in thanks as they made their way to the center of the spaceport.

When they reached the control room, they were brought before a figure Nestor didn't recognize, immediately, as Di Mon. He stood running a hand over a nervecloth sheet mounted on a floor-standing frame, face pinched with exhaustion and his usually immaculate clothing disordered, as if he hadn't changed it, or slept, for too long.

Before the commander could finish introducing his prisoners, Di Mon whirled on them.

"Where are their clothes?" he shouted.

"My Liege, we were worried they would try to poison you," the commander said, bowing gently.

"Poison me? This man is more loyal to me than *you*, you brainless parochial— never mind. Get them clothes and don't speak to me again until you've redirected blood flow to your brain." He shot hot glares at the male and female guard who hadn't quite detached their stares from the naked condition of their prisoners. "All of you!"

The commander opened his mouth, then walked out. When the guards accompanying Nestor and Remei made no motion to leave, Di Mon surged toward them, striking one hard in the face.

"In case it wasn't clear, I do not need your *protection*," he spat. "Get out!" he said, shoving the nearest guard in the direction of the door.

The rest of the guards scurried out of the room, faces red and heads bowed.

Di Mon slammed the door and turned slowly toward Nestor and Remei. His face looked stricken with grief and an inner conflict Nestor could only guess at. He closed his eyes and rubbed them with thumb and forefinger, stopping all movement as though he could remain in that position for the rest of time. Remei eyed the makeshift bed, in one corner. Nestor gave her a slight nod. She darted over to pull a sheet and coverlet off the bed, wrapping herself in one and carrying the other back to Nestor where he stood, watching their troubled host.

The control room was on the top floor of the spaceport, and the windows at Di Mon's back looked out onto the landscape of the city and untouched fields. From this vantage point it hardly seemed like any war was going on. Inside the control room were signs Di Mon had been camping out here. The control panels had been made into desks for Green Hearth staff, and nervecloth screens set up here and there. In addition to the bed Remei had raided, a change of clothes hung in one corner.

Di Mon opened his eyes and looked at them with a grim face. "Tell me everything," he said.

Chapter 12

"What happened, my little friend?" said Prokhor, his face a twisted mess of confusion as he stared at a quaking and crying Voltan.

"They— they weren't there," Voltan said, balling his hands into fists as he lifted his shoulders and tightened his body. "Nobody was."

"Where, home?"

Voltan frowned, ignoring the queer face that Prokhor made when he was concerned. "The sanctuary. Where Remei lived. She and Nestor were supposed to be there to take care of us. They weren't supposed to let us out of their sight."

Prokhor flinched. "They shirked their responsibilities," he said, with a sagacious nod. "It is truly a challenge to find someone on whom you can depend in such trying times."

Voltan gave him a disgusted look. "They all abandoned me. Including my sister."

"I am sorry," Prokhor said, closing his eyes and stepping closer to the boy. "I wish I could help you find them, if only to shake them by the tunic and help sharpen their empathy, but my duties require me to stay here."

Voltan blinked through his tears, sniffling. "Your research is that important?"

Prokhor's face grew serious. "Oh yes, quite." He looked at the table where the protein visualizer lay. "You know, my research was one of the ways that I learned to cope with my own parents abandoning me."

A lengthy silence filled the small room as Voltan stared at living proof that maybe he could, after all this was over, still grow up to be a whole and healthy Gelack. Prokhor's similarity to himself also frightened him, because it closed off the unknowable that allowed his childish dreams to blossom and remain untouched by the horror surrounding them. Tangible possibility could teeter too close toward the realities he tried to shut from his mind.

His fear caved to the desire of curiosity. "Y—your parents abandoned you?"

Prokhor nodded, his lips pursed as he held Voltan's gaze. "They were pulled in different directions, and I got lost in the middle. My father was a Lorel, and my mother Vrellish. Their union was abhorred by both. The Vrellish shunned my mother for choosing such a partner. She loved my father— as a *mekan'st* or a *cher'st*? I don't know. It doesn't matter. Trying to walk the thin line and maintain family ties was too much for both of them."

Voltan's brow furrowed as he tried to weigh the act of abandonment against any list of external pressures. "But why couldn't they take you with them?"

"They split up and fled. Both feared for their lives. The Lorels seemed the most likely candidates capable of raising me without hatred or scorn." Prokhor's face darkened, his eyelids drooping as his lips sneered. "What neither my mother nor my father foresaw or realized was how arrogant the Lorels are."

Voltan's eyes widened. He hadn't fully realized, until now, what the implications of being raised by Lorels might be. "What did they do to you?"

"They weren't overtly cruel, necessarily. I was just the dumb bastard child that everyone felt sorry for, and was held back from the full privileges that most Lorels are afforded." Voltan watched Prokhor's arm tense in a strange manner that made it seem disjointed.

"What privileges?" Voltan asked.

Prokhor looked at him sideways, smiling sardonically. "Well, let's just say that they do more than hold Demish dinner parties."

Voltan stared at Prokhor's arm, wondering what sort of things the Lorels might have done to his friend just because Prokhor's mother and father couldn't handle the pressure of parenthood. "Do you still talk to the Lorels?" he asked.

"On occasion. I have to," he said, turning to pace the length of the room. He came back to Voltan and crouched down, putting his hands on the boy's shoulders. "But between you and me, my friend, they don't know about this research."

The conspiratorial glint in Prokhor's eyes made Voltan gulp. He thought of the harsh treatment the Lorels gave the man in front of him based solely on his mixed heritage, and his face hardened. "I won't tell anyone."

Prokhor's eyebrows lifted. "Thank you, Voltan."

Voltan's face reddened, and he stared at his feet, kicking minute flecks of dust across the floor.

Prokhor went to a cabinet in the far corner of the room, opened it with a key, and pulled out a cage which he set on the pristine white countertop. "Do you want to know the most important facet of my research?"

Voltan looked up, acknowledging that he had been watching Prokhor, and nodded vigorously.

"The takoshi," Prokhor said proudly, opening the cage and letting a quarter-meter-long lizard-like animal trot out onto the counter. It had marble-sized eyes and a set of massive claws on its front legs. The takoshi squatted on large-muscled stumpy back legs. Its skin was ribbed and flecked with textured spots where the light-blue skin was darker.

"That's just like Enid's!" exclaimed Voltan, and upon seeing Prokhor's dark, puzzled expression, became subdued. "Well, sort of. His is red and the feet are different, I think."

Prokhor's lips shook slightly, and Voltan could see his jaw tighten for a few moments. "Oh," he said after some time, "you've seen a takoshi before, have you?"

Voltan swallowed. "I think so. It's hard to tell. Enid called his Cam."

Prokhor's gaze lowered as he nodded slowly. "Enid is Nestor and Remei's child, yes?"

Voltan nodded, a tremor of anxiety nesting in his stomach.

"Astonishing," Prokhor said, brow furrowed. "I wonder where they got the creature."

Voltan shifted, feeling awkward about the reaction his mention of Enid's pet had caused. "So they're the most important part?" he ventured. "Of your research?"

Prokhor straightened, coming back from the far-off gaze that had taken possession of his face. "Yes. They are the focus of everything."

Voltan reached out a tentative finger toward the takoshi. "What's his name?"

Prokhor raised an eyebrow, glancing between Voltan and the lizard.

"Didn't you give him one?" Voltan said, frowning. "He must be really young then."

Prokhor's expression was flat. "Yes."

"Okay." Voltan set his hand on his chin in a thoughtful manner. "What does he do? What are his habits?"

Prokhor stared at the takoshi blankly for a moment. "He tears through hullsteel with his claws."

Voltan's jaw dropped. "What!? Nothing does that! Nothing but shakeups, then it shatters!" He blinked at the takoshi. "It's a wonder that he hasn't torn through his cage," he said, in wonder.

"He… likes his cage."

Voltan nodded, lips together. "All right. Since he can do something as legendary as tear hullsteel, he needs a hero-like name. Like in the old legends I read about in…" His face flushed. "It's probably a stupid name."

"No," Prokhor said carefully. "It's better than no name. And I'm a fan of those legends."

"The Tideripper," Voltan said, a brief flicker of confidence before he lowered his head again. "Or Tye for short."

Prokhor smiled. "Quite an appropriate name."

"Why do you need to cut hullsteel so badly?"

"I don't need to cut hullsteel. The Lorels developed the venom in his claws to sabotage hullsteel in its pre-casting state, so it will be vulnerable to specific Lorel tactics when it is the skin of a Sevolite battlewheels. Making them easy to shatter." He blinked as he scanned Voltan's body for a reaction.

"That's awful." Voltan's face soured. "Everyone would die of depressurization. It's *okal'a'ni.*"

"I agree," Prokhor said, running his strange hand over the scaled spine of the takoshi. "The Lorels had all kinds of

plans for the takoshi. Ways to use them as means of deliver-
ing deadly payloads or spy on their Sevolite masters once
they managed to get them accepted as high status pets— the
way cats were, once. That's why I want to learn to control
them."

Voltan paused for a moment. "So you can stop them from
doing too much damage?"

Prokhor nodded. "So we can have a defense against
them."

Taking Tideripper in his arms, Voltan gave Prokhor a
serious look. "How do we start?"

Di Mon rubbed his forehead as he sat opposite Nestor
across a table strewn with nervecloth components. He
turned the broadcasting nervecloth over in his hands, the
muffled voice coming from it tainting the silence before he
spoke.

"I don't know, yet, how Kai'til's managed to make so
many people lose every scrap of their sanity," he told them.
"But he's done it. He's rabid himself. His propaganda
claims he's protecting me from disgrace at court by keeping
me ignorant of the tactics he's using to clean up. But I think
he's on the brink of open mutiny. I know he has henchmen
who are telling him I'm the mastermind behind the whole
doping scandal, to increase the highborn population of
Monatese." He looked at Nestor and Remei. "They are looking for an excuse to try to kill me before the reinforcements
get through. It would be a tactical error for me to oppose
them openly, before I can win the fight."

Dressed, now, in their original clothes, Nestor had torn
his pant-leg off and Remei was in the process of removing
the bullet from his calf. Her husband winced with each tiny
movement of her tweezers, closing his eyes with his neck
arched in subdued pain. "Yes," he said, groaning. "They
will find an excuse to walk over you."

"We must find a compromise," Di Mon said, standing
up and beginning to pace. "Somewhere between what they
want and how I want them all dead."

Remei pulled out the bullet, eliciting a cry from Nestor.
She dropped it onto the table beside her with a *clunk*. It

created a blood-pool where it touched. Heaving a sigh of relief, she wiped her forehead with the back of her hand. "We don't want all the militia dead," she said. "Just Kai'til. Cut off the head, preferably his."

"How could so many be manipulated like this?" Di Mon growled, squeezing the nervecloth in his fist. "They're Monatese, not some priest-blinded Nesaks!"

Remei froze with a seamer in her hand and stared at him. "Excuse me?"

"Not you," Di Mon said hurriedly, dismissing her offended look with a wave of his hand. "And you know what I mean. They're following too easily."

Nestor looked at Remei's seamer with a mixture of fatigue and anxiety in his eyes. "You don't have to twist their arms too hard to encourage the prejudices that *Okal Rel* instills."

"*Okal Rel* does not encourage random shootings and razing peaceful neighborhoods!" snapped Di Mon.

"The prejudices of Gelack society, then, if you're being picky. Ow!" Nestor sucked in a breath as Remei began working the wound closed with her seamer.

Di Mon stared out the window at the green fields and the streets of the city that told nothing of the suffering that was happening everywhere. Time stretched with only the sound of Remei's seamer working away. Nestor briefly wondered how he would get out of the spaceport without being killed, particularly if Di Mon himself knew his authority was stretched thin.

"Exodus," Di Mon said quietly, his voice laden with sadness and disappointment.

"What's that?" asked Remei.

"Exodus. We have to take the illegally-enhanced families off-planet."

"Will that satisfy the thirst for blood?" asked Nestor.

"I think it has to," replied Di Mon, rubbing his chin. "They want a pure society, and the removal of the 'mold' will give them just that. Of course, they'll want a provable way to ensure that all the 'abominations' are removed. And it may be harder to protect the guilty parents than the innocent children."

Nestor gave his friend a sideways glance, nodding despite the pain lacing up his leg. "Di Mon, do you think there's a potential benefit to Monitum in these extra high-borns?"

"Don't tell me you just realized that," said the liege of Green Hearth, giving Nestor a tired look.

"No, I just didn't know if you were for or against it."

"Does it matter?" continued Di Mon. "It would be incredible if Monitum could produce highborns in such a manner, but that's just the problem. It's not credible. It would be like counterfeiting honor chips and expecting to profit by it in the long run. The Silver Demish would unite with the Red Vrellish and Nersallians to overrun us once we dropped the shield of honor. Fountain Court is always watching for Monitum to prove it can't be trusted."

Nestor's brow furrowed. "You think this is a setup?"

"I think this whole thing smells bad," Di Mon said, darkly.

"But if the bloodshed could be quenched, and the bio-science behind it made acceptable, wouldn't it be a huge gift to Monitum to be handed lots of highborns for generations to come?"

Di Mon shook his head, eyes closed. "Quenched? Accepted?" He rubbed his hands together and crossed his arms. "Sevildom will not accept them. Because in the end, they cheated. And there is no greater hatred, Nestor, than that of a man who played by the rules and lost to a cheater. Whether you accept those rules or not according to your personal philosophy, a society's rules express a working compromise between its members about an acceptable way to vie for power. Break them, and you fling open the doors to chaos." He paused before adding, coldly, "Take what you've seen here, today, and multiply it across every planet in the empire. Not to mention…" His jaw locked as he looked away. Nestor thought he might say more, but the muscles along Di Mon's jawline only tightened.

The spaceport's hollow interior produced gentle echoes of the industry and the many people who filled it— echoes that magnified in the silence as Nestor, Remei and Di Mon sat there, still and exhausted. Several minutes passed before

Nestor heaved a sigh that barely rose above the whispers of the building. "So how are we going to get everyone off?"

"I'll round them up with my most trusted officers," Di Mon said. "Although I'm not sure whether that means anything anymore," he muttered to himself, then looked up at Nestor. "You know where they are?"

"The refugees? No, I didn't want Olivia and everyone to feel trapped in one location should they need to stay on the move."

Di Mon frowned. "I can't use the general population to help out, and I'm reluctant to engage more out-of-province people in this mess, now, given the damage control I'll have to manage afterwards. I don't know if I could control the backlash, in either direction, if what was happening here became more widely known."

He fixed Nestor with a steely look. "I will help the refugees," he told him. "But whatever is going on here has to be contained as much as possible. And the sooner the better. So if you know where to find them, let's go get them."

"I know where Olivia's likely to be," Nestor said. "If we leave soon we won't have that much ground to cover."

"We'll load them on my personal carrier and take them to Sanctuary — the planet Sanctuary, I mean — until we have the time to sort out a solution."

"What about the missing children?" Remei murmured.

"Sorry, Remei?" Nestor asked.

"Enid and Voltan," she said again. "What are we going to do about them?"

The thought of going alone back into the fray after the children made Nestor sick with exhaustion. He liked the idea of fighting off the evil with Di Mon's help— it shared the load and increased the chances of success. But Enid was his son! How could he have forgotten him?

"We can't search for a couple of strays," Di Mon cut in before Nestor could answer. "The priority is to get the refugees off, then the situation will stabilize."

Remei's face held an expression of barely contained fury. "And in the meantime, we just pray they 'strays' will do fine on their own? Enid and Voltan were either kidnapped or have run away together. Nestor and I barely made it this far, and it was only a day's travel. You expect them to stand a fighting chance?" She turned to Nestor. "Tell him to give us troops!"

"My love—" Nestor began.

"I can't commit additional resources when so much is at stake. Something is drastically *wrong* here. With all of this. I am already making a concession to compassion by diverting my loyalist errants to rescue people already grouped together."

"Nestor! Do you agree with him?" Remei cried.

Nestor swallowed thickly, looking at the floor of the spaceport. There was some sense to Remei's argument, and he too wanted the children back. But the military part of him could not justify it. Whether it was that, or the fact that he couldn't bear the idea of another solo struggle, he couldn't tell, and the guilt twisted his stomach like a mess of shorted nervecloth wire. "The faster we get everyone off-planet, the safer Monitum will be for everyone," he said quietly.

Remei's jaw dropped as she inhaled sharply, and took a step back.

"Remei, I want the children back as—"

"All right," she said, holding up her hand as she walked to the door. She let out a heavy sigh, her exhalation the only sound in the room, dwindling into the buzz of lighting. Her shoulders drooped and she looked as though she were longing for the safe comfort of SanHome, her Nesak home world. A moment later her expression sharpened as if a visitation from the Watching Dead had brought her back from a far-off plane. "You're right. I'm just frustrated... but I understand." She closed her eyes. "I need to step out for a bit."

Nestor felt relief wash over him, the tangle inside unfurling as his whole body unclenched. A few seconds later, his brow furrowed as he recognized the familiar sharpening of tone at the end of her speech— like that time she had told him Cam the takoshi was no more, only to find out later that Enid had disguised him as a grab rat.

"Gods," he said, rising and bolting out the door after her. She was already rounding the corner at the end of the hallway when he got there. He raced through the passageways, but soon lost sight of her.

"Have you seen my wife?" he asked a nearby guard.

The guard blinked. Monatese commoners persisted in the tradition of marriage, but 'wife' it was an odd thing to hear from a highborn with Vrellish coloring. "The Nesak?"

"Yes!"

The guard shook his head.

Nestor turned to see Di Mon walking toward him. "Nestor, I can't do this without you," he said.

"Can you search for her?" Nestor asked the guard, his voice croaking. "At least for the next hour?"

Di Mon put a hand on his shoulder. "After that, we must leave," he said. His voice was tender and his face betrayed some of the agonizing political pressure he felt. "If she returns she will be safe here."

Nestor closed his eyes, a tear spilling over and down his cheek.

Chapter 13

"We are smarter, faster, and stronger than they are," Pleo said, pacing the ranks of boys and girls who stood in three neat lines. Behind him knelt an older man, tied and gagged. "We can hide better, get the jump on them and hit them hard." With each word he spoke, his confidence rose. He had found himself addicted to the intoxicating taste of command and authority, and it seemed to mask the ugly pain that crept in when he wasn't doing something.

"Di Mon has offered us 'abominations' a free pass off-planet!" declared Pleo. "But do we want to be torn from our homes? Do we accept never seeing justice enacted for the attacks we have suffered?"

"*No!*" shouted the children in unison.

"Should we pay the price of what our fathers have done to us?"

"*No!*"

"Are you going to sit back and do nothing?"

"*NO!*"

Pleo's face was grim, but it took great effort to mask the smile he felt. "The majority of the guilty adults will be on the passenger ship that Liege Monitum intends to load. That is because, my brothers and sisters, we have done tremendous work showing that we will not forgive the way they betrayed everything *Okal Rel* stands for.

"We have cornered the rats, and they will fight harder than ever. Grouped in one place, they will at once be hard and easy to kill. Easy because we need not go hunting for them in different locations, but difficult because they will possess strength in numbers and have the protection of Green Hearth's errants working for Liege Monitum.

"We must prepare, brothers and sisters, for a final fight. The training I must ask of you will stretch the limits of your abilities, but your fortitude has given me great confidence. And remember, we have one tremendous weapon that the enemy will not expect when they load the passenger ship. My father practically rebuilt the spaceport, and I know it better than anyone."

Pleo finally allowed the smile to emerge, a wicked grin that caught like a virus through the ranks. He walked over in front of Enid, and put a hand on the boy's shoulder. At first Enid had tried to avoid eye contact, but as Pleo stared at him, he couldn't help but return the gaze. The subordinate boy started to tremble as Pleo's grin turned into a sneer.

"Before we continue training, we must take care of our garbage," he said, looking at the man behind him tied and gagged on the ground. "Enid Tark, are you ready to do your part?"

Silence answered Pleo, with all the children looking timidly toward Enid, who stared at the ground. "It's against *Okal Rel*," he said after some time.

"*Okal Rel* is about respect for the environment, and these traitors have shown complete disregard for it." Pleo took a few steps toward Enid. Cam the takoshi, standing on Enid's shoulder, began to growl.

"You are killing them in a dishonorable way," Enid said, raising his gaze briefly. "They don't have a chance to fight back."

"Why should we afford them honor, when they are honor-less?" Pleo asked. He turned and extended his question to his crowd of followers. "Did they show us the same respect when they tried to hunt us down?"

"No," muttered Enid.

"They are the cause of this war, and in order to hide from their responsibilities and save their skins, they have sided with other bloodthirsty hypocrites who think children are to blame." Pleo's nostrils flared. "How like a coward to hunt children." He turned and gave a sharp kick to the chest of the kneeling man, knocking him to the ground.

"Enid, this world is full of cowards and liars who don't stand for anything, who switch teams when it's convenient for them. Who refuse to do what's necessary to bring about peace."

"I'm not a coward," Enid said, arms tightening against his sides.

"Then show me you have what it takes to apply justice in this terrible place. Show everyone you have the strength to help us rebuild society, and restore *Okal Rel* once more."

Whoops and cheers rang out through Pleo's followers.

"Are we not being hypocrites, abusing the principles of *Okal Rel* principles to take vengeance?" Enid whispered, his voice nearly lost to the rising cacophony of the child soldiers.

"Quiet!" Pleo shouted angrily, hushing and frightening every wide-eyed boy and girl. "Enid has brought up a good question. Are we as bad as the enemy for forsaking *Okal Rel* while we carry out justice?" He allowed himself to pause, and saw how Enid was now hanging on his every word. Pleo's shoulders lifted up and back as he leaned in. "The enemy is hoping that we will try to apply the old principles in response to their betrayal. They are relying on us to react the way they expect us to, and not to make a decision.

"But can principles of honor be applied to someone who wrecks a space station with a *rel*-fighter? Can you do a shimmer dance that says, 'Please, sir, let us fight like gentlemen!' and expect him to comply? No, you cannot. And we cannot apply *Okal Rel* to the traitors for the same reason. They would destroy us through their lack of loyalty and principles.

"But unlike them, my brothers and sisters, we have not forgotten where our hearts really lie. When all this is over, we will once more have a society that our grandparents would be proud of. We will have peace." Pleo felt the words roll off his tongue as his excitement fed off the bobbing heads in the crowd of children. *And Mother, you will finally be able to rest,* he thought. *And come back into this world from the Watching Dead, where we can be a family once more.* He felt a pang in his chest at the thought of Olivia and Voltan on the run, alone; or even being escorted off-planet with the other children of modified parents. He wished they could see him, now. See what he offered and how he brought hope to Grianach.

Sigurd stood up and clapped him on the back. "Three cheers for Pleo!"

Amidst the *hoorays* Pleo saw that Enid was looking at him with admiration, although he hadn't opened his mouth.

"Enid!" he said in a commanding voice, interrupting the chanting. "Help us bring peace." He grabbed a sword lying against a nearby tree and unsheathed it, extending the handle toward Enid. The rest of the child warriors broke rank and began to surround the bound man, watching Enid earnestly.

Enid stared at Pleo for a few seconds before reaching out a hand and grabbing the handle. The man on the ground writhed and mumbled, but a few kicks from the surrounding boys stifled his cries. Enid stood over the man, the noise in the air a contagious vector of bloodlust. Pleo placed his hands on Enid's shoulders, and whispered, "You are doing a great thing, Enid Tark."

The chants from the boys and girls rose to a deafening level, until Pleo felt lost in a wave of energy that nothing could stop. His vision began to blur and he sensed a clear dream coming on. Images of his mother and father in the amphitheater flashed in his head, and screeching static-filled bursts of noise beat through his eardrums.

Pleo fell to his knees on the ground, the noise transforming into a thousand shuttles taking off out of his father's spaceport. His brother and sister hopped from wing to wing as he watched the spectacular show.

When Pleo awoke, Sigurd was at his side, holding him by the shoulder as Pleo took in gasping breaths. The child soldiers had all grabbed Enid and were tossing him in the air. A few meters from Pleo lay the man, a sword plunged through his heart.

Olivia took a seat beside Faren on the grassy hillside away from the makeshift tents and shelters that the refugees had thrown up in the surrounding woods. It was dusk. Soon it would be cooling off and growing dark.

Exhaling loudly, she felt throbbing tension in her shoulders from all the work that she had done in order to try and make acceptable living arrangements for everyone. The injured among those who had fought back at the house couldn't move well enough to do it, and had been too proud to ask for help.

"Should be it," she said, exhaustion making her eyelids heavy.

"You're amazing," said Faren, his pale face lit dimly by nearby lamps. "I can't believe how much you've done."

"I couldn't have done it without help. Without *your* help."

Faren looked down at his feet. Olivia couldn't tell if he was blushing or not. "I never realized how much I took my parents' place for granted," he confessed. "The chandeliers, the decorations, all seemed commonplace and I told myself it didn't matter what was in my house. But the truth is, I miss it." He stole a glance back at the asymmetrical, hastily-cobbled bivouacs that dotted the landscape behind them.

"We do the best we can," Olivia replied. "Maybe we'll make you a chandelier out of twigs tomorrow." She poked him softly.

Faren laughed. "It's good that I don't have a chandelier. I'll have to get used to it, because I don't think my father will take me back now that I've been spotted with the refugees."

Olivia stared at him and wondered how any parent could harbor hatred or shame for his child, when the time families had together was so fleeting. She wondered if it would be worse to have a dead parent, or one she could never see or talk to. "I'm sorry."

Faren blinked. "No, it's all right. We were never... close. Besides, it's given me a chance to grow. To learn how to appreciate other things." He smiled, extending his hand to touch her leg.

Olivia felt the nerves in her skin sharpen in sensitivity, and she tried to hide a small gasp as the touch sent jolts of electricity through her body. "Faren, I... now's not..." Her voice trailed off, her thoughts a jumbled mess.

"So much has happened," he said softly, "that no one's had any time to absorb any of it."

Olivia's lips trembled, and she put her hand on Faren's, which sent a whole new array of sensations through her, while providing a strangely calming effect. "I... appreciate everything that you've done, Faren."

He wrapped his fingers around hers. "It was nothing."

Her heart echoing in her ears, she looked down as the words tumbled out of her. "I like you, but I don't think now's the right time to do anything about... us. It wouldn't be right to start something when so many people need us. We have to make sure everyone's safe, and take care of them." She stared at the ground and wished that she could bury her head in the dirt to avoid seeing Faren's reaction. Her hand trembled as she waited for him to snatch his away, to reject her, to say she was inhibited and un-Vrellish.

His hand didn't move, but she couldn't tell if her own shaking had increased or if he had added to it. "When will there be a... right time, Olivia?"

She closed her eyes, not wanting to project into the future. She could hardly see past the next meal, when motherless children and weak adults would need to be fed on whatever they happened to scrounge off the land, since their supplies were dwindling. In the long-term she hoped for a peaceful time, with Mom and Dad back somehow — miraculously — and the whole family together, but the path to get there was completely out of reach. "Not for a while," she admitted sadly.

"A lot might happen between now and then, to both of us," said Faren, turning his body toward hers.

"Don't say that," she said, frowning then averting her eyes.

"I didn't mean it that way... just that there might never be a right time."

She pulled her hand off her knee and shoved his away, turning on him. "What do you want me to say, Faren? What do you want from me? I'm giving everything I have right now and have nothing left." She felt the weight of everything in the pits of her eyes, in her chest and shoulders, making her want to curl into a ball and never awaken.

"I don't want anything from you," he whispered, his face a mixture of fear and longing. "I just want to give you my love."

From any other Vrellish boy, Olivia would have thought Faren had meant something physical, but the look on his face told her otherwise. "I'll make a terrible partner," she told him.

"You're already wonderful the way you are," he assured her.

Olivia cast her head down, unfamiliar how to react to anything but the pain and anger that had swamped her life for what felt so long. She still wasn't sure what he meant, or what he wanted. *Ask me for food, shelter, care, attention— anything else,* she thought.

She felt his hands touch her back as he moved behind her and began massaging her shoulders. She tensed up, shrugging her shoulders as a chill ran through her.

"It's okay, Olivia. It's me," said Faren.

"I'm afraid you won't want me if I let you in," she blurted out, a tremor passing across her back.

"Nothing could ever make me turn from you," he said soothingly, his breath sending wisps of air across her neck.

"You don't know what's inside," she said pleadingly. "I don't even know."

"I think we've both demonstrated that we can handle any secrets your insides may hold," he said, poking her in the stomach. "And the last one was a pretty big one, too."

She craned her neck to look at him. *His support has never wavered, even though it would have been much easier and safer for him to follow his parents' wishes,* she thought. "All right, so if a little takoshi starts growing in my stomach, you won't be grossed out?" she asked.

"What, like that thing Enid had? I will raise him as my own," he said with mock nobility, straightening and putting a hand across his chest. "I will teach him the ways of honor and all the subjects that you would have him learn."

"I'm not sure a takoshi would be able to absorb it all."

"Well, we can try."

Olivia leaned in and pulled him closer to her. "And if I start growing scales later?"

Faren looked up thoughtfully. "Well, I suppose it depends *where* the scales start growing…"

She punched him in the stomach, making him gag as he started laughing. "You're just like any other Vrellish boy."

His face grew serious as he leaned toward her. "No, I'm not." He pushed his lips against hers softly, the sensations pulsing through her nerves as Faren kissed her again and again, putting a hand on her cheek.

When he pulled away and they both opened their eyes, Faren wore a smile that quickly transformed into concern for Olivia's reaction.

She grabbed his head with both arms and pulled him toward her as his eyebrows lifted in surprise. They fell to the grass with their lips together.

The frantic urgency that had punctuated their many recent flights repeated itself in their lovemaking as they yanked each other's clothes off and embraced. The dammed-up, emotional energy spilled over as they surged together. The release of all concern felt liberating and empowering, a peculiar strength found by exposing weakness.

"I love you," said Faren in between pants. "I love you."

Olivia melted into him and several minutes later they lay breathing against one another, sweat forming a warm film that joined most of their torso and legs.

Any sense of time had been completely lost. To Olivia, it seemed like they had just been there a few minutes before a loud voice shattered their sanctuary. "Olivia! Are you there? Olivia?"

She scrambled for her clothes, scanning the area to see if anyone could see her. She slipped her tunic and pants on rapidly, and began lacing them up. The sweat of her passion now felt like icicles on her skin. "Yes, what is it?"

"There are some soldiers approaching," said the voice, and she could see a pale-faced boy named Tral walking out from the line of tents.

She raced over and gripped him by the shoulder. "Where?"

Tral pointed to the eastern edge of their tent line, and she pulled him with her as she sprinted. Again, she wondered if she would find Pleo among the troops searching for the refugees. Maybe he could once again save them or give them some time to escape. She tried not to think about the possibility that he would be forced to attack. She shivered and tugged her tunic tighter with crossed arms.

Twenty or so lamps lit the path through the forest that led to their encampment, and Olivia cursed as she peered over the hillside lying flat on her stomach. That many *okal'a'ni* warriors could easily level the refugees if they were willing to use the right weaponry. "Wake everyone. Tell them to be silent and ready to run," she said.

Tral bowed and scampered off, ducking until he was sufficiently far away.

Faren touched her shoulder and whispered, "I'll help him."

"Thank you," she breathed, wishing she could freeze time or pass over the war. She hated how rapidly the world could be turned upside down. Again.

She stared at the line of approaching lights and wondered how likely it was that the troops had spotted her settlement. If they had, they were awfully overconfident, moving at a slow pace. Maybe they would just walk right by, without cresting the rise of the hill and coming into the glen...

Too late. They turned and began coming straight toward her. They would be here in less than ten minutes. Pushing back and getting up, hunched over to stay low, she ran to the other edge of the camp, thinking how difficult it would be to move through the dense forest behind them without making a great deal of noise.

She watched the villagers jump out of their tests, chests heaving as adrenaline jolted them brutally awake. They stared at her, some shivering, others with eyes so wide she thought they would pop out of their skulls.

"We might have to fight them," she said in a whisper, pacing around and scanning everyone's reaction as they emerged from their shelters to face the center of the encampment. She hoped it was dark enough they couldn't see her blood-drained face.

"We haven't enough weapons," someone complained.

"They'll just shoot us—"

"Quiet," said Olivia, strength rising within her at each word of opposition. *Bless the gods for the places they hide virtue,* she thought as she scanned the waking crowd. "We will sneak into the forest away from the camp, and leap on them from the bushes with our swords. It's the only chance we stand. Anyone without a weapon should come and be ready to use every tool you have to hit them where it hurts."

She pointed to herself to indicate spots where the soldiers might be easily incapacitated.

"But what if—"

"Enough," she snapped. "We move. Now. There's no time. The signal to attack will be Tral at the top of the hill who will shout when he sees them. That will make them think we are still in the camp. Faren, you take that half, I'll take this half."

They snuck to the edges of the tent area and began creeping down the hill, crawling through bushes as the lights rose steadily toward them. Olivia clutched the sword awkwardly as she took her place between two bushes. *Please don't be Pleo,* she prayed. *Please, Gods, let Pleo not be among them.*

Tral shouted from atop the hill, and Olivia sprang to action, hearing those around her do the same. She leapt out of the bushes and raised the sword to strike. She surged toward a man with his back turned, until at the last instant he turned with his sword centimeters from her throat.

It was Nestor. Leaning backward and slipping on the wet ground, she screamed. Nestor, wide-eyed, barely slowed his swing down in time to miss her, and a moment later he had dropped his sword. The sound of grunts and swords clashing sounded all around them.

"Stop!" shouted Olivia. "They're not enemies! Stop! Stop! STOP!"

It took a few seconds for the bloodlust to quiet, as everyone stared at each other in confusion. Nestor reached down and helped Olivia up. His strong hand reminded her of her father, and for once the memory didn't invoke pain.

"Thank the Watching Dead," Nestor whispered.

"Who are these people!?" shouted a refugee.

"I am your liege," said Di Mon, his voice silencing all the whispering and arguing voices.

"And we are friends," said Nestor, keeping his eyes fixed on Olivia as he smiled. "Here to help you."

Hushed amazement rippled through the crowd. Olivia struggled to speak, her throat tight with a mixture of worry and shame at the realization of what she'd almost done. Instead, she threw her arms out and hugged Nestor. "Does this mean it's over?" she managed to ask after a while.

Nestor patted her back without answering for a few minutes. Finally, Olivia pried herself loose and looked him squarely in the eyes. "Did you find Voltan and Enid? What's happening, Nestor?"

He took a deep breath and shook his head, lowering his eyes. He paused before he met her gaze again. "We're going to take the refugees off-planet to Sanctuary."

Chapter 14

Voltan stared at the complex web of jagged, interconnected links and loops that made up the protein, and squeezed it once more between his virtual fingers. Smiling, he spun and zoomed in, weaving through the structure one more time, this time just enjoying the ride. He imagined wind blowing on his face as he soared through the chemical landscape.

He took off the hood. "I've got it," he said.

Prokhor stood up abruptly, his arm swinging strangely asynchronously and out of rhythm to his steps as he scurried over to him. "You have, have you?"

"Yes," Voltan said, nodding his head sagely. "There's no other way the structure could perform as it does, or react the way it does with the data you've given me."

"Let me see."

Voltan let Prokhor try the hood on, passing him the gloves. Prokhor spent several minutes poking and prodding in mid-air, and Voltan wondered if he'd looked that strange, himself, when he was using it. It didn't matter much either way— he had had way too much fun doing it.

"Mad Gods," said Prokhor in an amazed voice, lifting the hood off. "You've done it."

Voltan felt a warm wave of pride as he sat up straighter and smiled. "It wasn't too bad. There were enough tests and criteria that I could pretty much just figure out one section at a time, piecing the information together." He made assembling motions with his hands.

"And well you did," Prokhor said, touching him on the shoulder with his strange arm flexing in an uncanny way. Voltan had to resist the urge to shirk away. "It's perfect, Voltan."

"So now that we know the structure of the dominant neurotransmitter in the takoshi, what next?"

"You waste no time, do you?" Prokhor said with a chuckle. "You could well be a Lorel yourself."

Voltan frowned. "I thought I was doing a good job."

"Oh you are, you are," Prokhor corrected quickly, seeing the disappointment on the child's face. "Not everything Lorels do is evil. They are incredible scientists, and you are proving to be quite a talented pupil, my little friend."

Voltan pursed his lips. "I don't ever want to do what they did with their power, though."

"Of course not," Prokhor soothed. "That is why you are stronger than they are." He beckoned Voltan over to a screen illuminated with scraggly lines beside a three-dimensional, semi-transparent map of a takoshi's brain. "Now we have to figure out how to mimic it, to manipulate them."

"Mimic the neurotransmitter?"

Prokhor nodded. "I've recorded electrochemical signals after giving the takoshi different suggestions, and am now confident in the following two patterns. This is what rejection looks like." The screen changed to light up with a colored series of pulses that stretched outward in a vast neural net in almost all areas of the brain. "And this is what acceptance looks like." The screen sent a different series of pulses, but Voltan couldn't tell exactly what the subtle differences were.

"Are the takoshi smart enough to take suggestions?" asked Voltan, bewildered at how the docile lizards could communicate with or understand Gelacks.

"You'd be surprised— there are creative ways of talking to them," said Prokhor. "We want their brains to light up like this—" He pointed at the 'acceptance' pattern. "—whenever they see *this*." The screen changed again. "A suggestion."

Voltan stared at the screen, trying to absorb the complexity of the task. "So we want to make the takoshi accept anything we suggest to them?" he ventured.

"Precisely."

Voltan stared at the pictures of acceptance and rejection, his mind flickering with ideas as to what protein structure might redirect the electrical impulses. He blinked several

times as the possibilities swam before him. Beneath everything, an overriding thought rose slowly to the surface,
shimmering into focus between bursts of protein images.

If I can control the takoshi, I can use them to fight back.

Remei floated like a dandelion seed in the wind, and
wove through the grip of Kai'til's forces. Her travelling
cloak and clothes were all she carried, but she found it easy
to slink in the spaces where people's attention waned and
find what she needed. On SanHome — her far-away Nesak
home world — the assumption that women were docile,
subservient family caretakers made her learn how to walk
the fine lines between perception and reality, skirting the
interleaved shadows to pursue her own ends.

Her first target was Paxasa, the broadcaster who spouted
out the toxic propaganda that sharpened hatred's blade.
She knew she couldn't fight the forces or kill Paxasa, but it
was the only place that might provide a clue to reaching the
source, the head of the serpent.

On SanHome there were episodes when broadcasting
took over the streets and invaded people's privacy. There
had been a time when loudspeakers all around the capitol
spouted sermons and prayer guides for the masses, until
an opposing order made those behind it stop. She had seen
one of the towers, and although she didn't fully understand
how it worked, she had a suspicion that Paxasa would need
a similarly tall building to broadcast.

The highest structure in the vicinity of the spaceport was
a grain refinery with tall silos that stretched high toward
the sky. Remei gazed upward, thinking that the reaches of
Sanctuary and Gelion — hours of *rel*-skimming travel time
away — were as isolated and distant as her missing children
were from her. She hugged the cloak around her as the wind
picked up, sending breaths of warm air up her legs and
around her torso. It seemed a bit too easy to think that the
heart of the broadcasting network lay right under Di Mon's
nose, but then again, he hadn't known about the broadcasts
until she and Nestor showed up. He'd also decided to make
the refugees his first priority, so the possibility could have
easily slipped past.

Her teeth chattering, she shook herself and continued on through the alleyway, pausing at the end as she watched guards stroll casually by. She wondered how many of them had seen her half-naked. Her jaw muscles tightened as the path forward opened once more. With an effortless and instinctive sense of where danger lurked, she pushed on toward the back of the refinery, watching as patrols passed up and down the passages she needed to penetrate.

She tried to keep focused on finding her way in, but her attention continued to drift toward thoughts of the children and the refugees. She blamed herself and Nestor for the disappearance of Enid and Voltan, but the crippling guilt would do them no good if she let it fully take hold. The journey had been manageable, but now that she was forced to sit idly and watch the refinery silos as people went in and out, she felt her body tremble.

I have to get in, she repeated to herself, closing her eyes for a few seconds. *That's it. That's all.* She shivered again as she thought of a man who wasn't Nestor touching her roughly if they found her. The pants she wore only half-fit and the vest was loose, so she was hoping that she would be able to hide her sex.

I should've taken Nestor's nervecloth ear piece, she thought, clenching her jaw in regret. It might have given her clues to what was happening.

She flinched as several air ships screamed past overhead, eliciting shouts and gestures from the nearby guards. What on Monitum could that mean? Was it Di Mon's escort to protect the passenger ship's lift-off, or was it Kai'til's ships, attacking Di Mon's? She listened to the sound of the engines fade into the distance.

One of the guards standing by an entryway beckoned to another passing by, and the two of them whispered conspiratorially. They both seemed focused on something one of them carried. After a few moments they walked off together, the entryway guard waving her hand dismissively as she glanced back one last time at the door.

The setting sun cast long shadows along the ground as Remei slid through the darkness, her travelling cloak rippling noiselessly about her. Crouched behind a freight container, she stared at the two guards who were off in their own dark corner with their backs turned. She prayed she wasn't as easily visible.

Taking a deep breath and gripping her cloak tightly, she dashed for the door, every small sound of her feet hammering in her ears. She didn't glance at the guards until she was at the door, and crept in, mouthing prayers that the door was well oiled. It was.

Inside, brightly lit hallways carried the voices and footsteps of people that seemed to come from a spiral staircase at the end. To either side were entrances to storage areas from which wafted the strong smell of cut grain.

The sounds carried well enough for her to understand. "Does he ever take breaks?" said a squeaky voice.

"He implements Kai'til's orders," replied a deeper, slower one.

"I've heard he thinks he's some sort of prophet."

"Are you always this dense when you've got a new posting? Hold your tongue before he hears you."

"He's so wrapped up in his speech that he'd never—"

A metal door opened and slammed. "Paxasa, sir."

"Get out," came the harsh, throaty voice of Paxasa. "Now."

"But sir—" said the squeaky one.

"You do not gossip about me when I am making an announcement," Paxasa declared. "And not while I can hear you."

The sounds of footsteps coming down the stairs made Remei dart inside one of the grain storage rooms. She listened in the darkness as the footsteps moved to the edge of the entryway, then out the door as it opened.

"Sir, Kai'til is going to do another formal announcement tomorrow," said the deeper voice.

Remei's heart skipped. *Here, tomorrow?*

"Again?" said Paxasa, exasperated. "The man doesn't know what his role in this war is, does he? I have to correct all his transcripts to make sure they have the right effect. Does his voice really carry more influence?"

There was a pause. "I'm not sure, sir. Those are just my orders."

Paxasa sighed. "Of course, of course. When is he coming by?"

"In the morning, I believe, sir. He wants to launch the attack on Di Mon soon, from what I understand, and needs to solidify his support base."

"Quite the theory," said Paxasa. "And probably correct. You're worth keeping around, Tilkato."

"My pleasure, sir."

"I can hear it now: 'Brothers and sisters, I stand as your devoted leader, betrayed by my own liege.' This is going to be fun."

Remei blinked a few times, fatigue setting in as stubbornly as if her task were complete and she had time to indulge in rest. She groaned inwardly, wishing for the strength to fight exhaustion.

Weariness hugged and pulled down on her features, feeling like a secondary presence that had been waiting in the shadows for the chance to pounce. *I'm not out yet,* she told herself, swallowing as she tried to hold her eyes open willfully. Her vision wavered.

Ensuring there was no one in the hallway, she peeked out and stared at the door. The two guards were now standing together at the doorway, chatting to one another. *Gods, when will you take a break?*

Hours passed, and when she nearly fell asleep standing up, she knew she wouldn't get out before she collapsed. Heading back into the storage room, she nestled herself in the hay at the far end of the storage bins, sharp bits of straw jutting into her everywhere. It almost felt like due punishment as she tried to get to sleep. The jagged grain scratched whenever she moved, and she found herself forcing her eyes shut, mouthing prayers for a bit of sleep.

I will get Kai'til tomorrow, she soothed herself. *I'll get him.*

The sun rose in the agricultural belt of Grianach district, far removed from all the turmoil that plagued the city. Pleo Ald'erda glared at Sigurd, who was halfway between sitting and lying down, with a cut lip and a fearful look in his eyes. Behind him, the band of children stood rigidly at attention, although they couldn't help but watch out of the corners of their eyes. Pleo's gaze darted to the airships parked nearby.

The previous day, he and all of the child warriors had snuck into the spaceport and snatched five airships. They had anticipated stealing six, but one group of boys failed to take off quickly enough, and had been captured by either Kai'til's militia or Liege Monitum's remaining loyalists—Pleo would never know which. It was a successful operation considering most of the children had never piloted, and had only heard descriptions of how it was done. The successful children's reaction to the loss of their friends made Pleo realize how unprepared they were for the final task that lay ahead, and how much more training they were going to need.

They could not afford to be children anymore.

"Where is your sword?" he shouted at Sigurd, finally offering an explanation for why he had struck him. He felt a stab of pain in his chest for the friend that cowered in front of him, but knew that he couldn't allow the transgression to pass.

"I— I don't know," Sigurd stammered.

"How will you fight anyone if you cannot keep track of your weapon?"

"It was an accident. There was so much going on!"

"Quiet!" Pleo kicked him in the ribs, pushing him onto his back. Sigurd erupted in a spasm of coughs. "That chaos was but a taste of what is to come. You said you were ready to fight for justice, but you can't hold onto your lifeline."

Pleo reached down, roughly flipped his friend onto his stomach and slashed at his tunic with the tip of his sword, slicing the fabric to reveal a bare, pale back. He addressed all the children. "Your sword is your only friend in battle. You have to be able to defend yourself. Without a sword you are nothing more than a helpless baby." He intended to teach the children how to fight without a sword, as well, and to use other weapons when they could find them. But he had to start somewhere to make the point.

He slashed a gash down Sigurd's shoulder all the way across his back to his hip. Sigurd screamed. Pleo winced, trying to mask the reluctance he felt. *He'll heal with his high-born physiology,* he thought.

"You will sleep beside your swords, and you will be ready to fight if I should wake you in the night. You are warriors now, and until the war is over, you will always be ready to fight— by night, by day."

Many of the children stared back at him with fierce determination in their eyes, the wide-eyed wonder disappearing slowly into the nether. "You will all have the chance to fly," he went on, "but only the best of you will fly in the end. Those of you who still have your swords are on the right path. You will now step forward, and remind Sigurd why he will never again lose sight of his blade."

He made a motion to indicate they were to slash Sigurd across his back, and saw some hesitate with sharp inhalations. There was a few seconds' pause, then a boy stepped forward with a lizard perched on his shoulder. It was Enid.

Enid strode to Sigurd's side, poked his sword just underneath the boy's shoulder blade until it drew blood, then slashed across. A few cheers rang through the ranks, and following Enid's example, more stepped forward.

Chapter 15

The passenger vessel lay with its belly in a now-charred field, the surrounding trees dwarfed by its massive grey bulk. Several on-ramps extended from the sides as supplies were loaded and people marshaled on. In an attempt to prevent Kai'til's people from infiltrating the ship, other refugees had to identify the person boarding.

Nestor paced at the top of one of the ramps, where he got a broader view of the large lines and slow-moving families. The identification process was time-consuming, but it was the only way to ensure the safety of the refugees. He felt uncomfortable with a pistol tucked into his vest, a precaution Di Mon thought necessary should the dishonorable try to put a stop to the ship. *Airships* patrolled the skies above — three of Di Mon's most trusted guards were all that could be spared. Five ships had been stolen the previous day, by unidentified raiders taking advantage of disintegrating order. The thought made Nestor rub his hands together nervously. Di Mon simply did not have the numbers to fight if the need arose, and as soon as the enemy realized that…

Olivia was moving quickly from line to line at the bottom of each ramp, helping families record details using either nervecloth or paper. She soothed tempers when people were outraged by the bureaucratic delays. Watching, Nestor found himself once more impressed by her tenacity and courage. Most children in her situation might have given in to despair, or abandoned everything in order to search for her two brothers. *No*, he thought, correcting himself. *Most people will never* be *in her situation*. Still, Olivia cared for and looked after the refugees with a determined look on her face that gave away no more than hints of the pain she must have felt.

Her anger had been ferocious when Nestor had told her that he and Remei had failed to find either of her brothers, but after the fire calmed — or had it just been tucked away? — she resolved to help get everyone off-planet.

Nestor put a hand to his ear, pushing the nervecloth into position. A soothing, classical Monatese sonata provided a soundtrack to the steady movement of people. He felt ill at ease, as though there should be more activity on the channel, more resistance to Di Mon's decree that the refugees be spared in exchange for accepting exile. Running his fingers along the hull of the transport, he took a deep breath. Despite the balmy sun he felt chilly from a bone-penetrating fatigue.

The sonata finished, and a familiar fanfare indicated that a message was about to be broadcast. The announcer came on. "Brothers and sisters, many of you are angry at our liege's decision to let the traitors go free to wreak their *okal'a'ni* terror on another planet, another system, another reach. I agree with you, and the time has come for action. I cannot underscore how important this moment is, nor how much courage will be required of each of you. For that reason, Damek Kai'til is here to make an announcement."

Nestor felt a lump form in his throat as he sucked in a breath.

"Greetings, good people of Grianach. Soldiers, warriors, devout followers of *Okal Rel*, I stand humbly before you on the edge of a precipice. The jump before us divides space and time into two paths, and never has the choice been more confusing.

"In ancient times, the Lorels used science to make puppets of Gelacks of all kinds, to pit them against each other. They were guilty of sacrilege of the body, mind and soul on top of all the sins they committed against the environment. They gave the word *okal'a'ni* its meaning.

"Now, centuries later, none of us are old enough to remember what the Lorels did. We forget why we have *Okal Rel* in the first place. We forget what it means to be honorable, to respect the environment. We take for granted the sacrifices that our ancestors made so that we could live a secure life where you have to back your word up with a sword.

"It's natural to want a better life, and after so much time without highborns, many of us are looking for other ways to strengthen Monitum. And so when someone comes along and offers you a needle and a better opportunity for your children, it's tempting. Even I might consider it, for I, like these sinners, am a nobleborn.

"But then I would remember *Okal Rel.* I would remember that my body is a sacred vessel through which I carry out my duties, my roles in the universe. To pervert our bodies is to deny the natural order of things, and our pact with the Watching Dead who are both our ancestors and will be our children, born again.

"If everyone were highborn, who would plough the fields and sow the grain? What would we eat? Sooner or later the jobs have to be done, and the real escape that people seek when they make themselves into abominations is one of labor. They are lazy and seeking the easy way out, rather than confront what is required of them.

"They claim to have done nothing wrong. That they are hurting no one. But their offspring will have an unfair advantage over your pure and natural children. And how can we know whether or not the Lorels control those children in some vile and secret manner? The very children who will rule over you.

"The destabilization of society is not something that will be broadcast on loudspeaker. It is not something that you will see until it is too late, and that is exactly what these *okal'a'ni* traitors are trying to do. They are destroying life as we know it, and they intend to destroy *us.*

"Di Mon has sided with them to allow them safe passage to Sanctuary. Should we allow them to pass unpunished from our grasp? Should we allow them to spread their tainted ways elsewhere, to destroy the way of life for everyone in their path? I think not. And, my brothers and sisters, I know that you also think not. To uphold what is right, sometimes you have to make a stand against authority.

"You have fought bravely up to this point, and for that you deserve the highest commendation. The spoils of war will be yours soon enough. I know some of you are tired, but you must trust me when I say that it is almost over. One more task I ask of you and it will end this rocky instability.

"Every able-bodied man, woman and child should come to the Grianach Arena in the capitol, where this journey began. We have captured a traitorous woman, and to inaugurate our final march toward justice and prosperity, we will show her that her ways will not be tolerated— not now, not ever. Now is the time for us to rise higher than we ever have before, and when this is done, we will hold our heads high in righteousness and earn the blessing of our ancestors."

Floating pollen in the air made Nestor's skin prickle as he tried not to imagine the crowds of listeners cheering at Kai'til's words. Or what they implied. His chest felt half-full of water, and he sucked in several shallow breaths as he stared at the slow-moving clouds wondering if something might appear out of them to prove to him that this was nothing more than fantasy. *To Hell with duty,* he thought, setting off down the ramp, his legs falling faster and faster before he nearly collided with the line of boarding passengers.

"Nestor!" shouted Olivia, whose voice seemed muffled and far away. "Where are you going?"

He slowed only because, after all she had done, she deserved an explanation.

"Remei," he said, panting as he turned and spotted her down the hill. "They have Remei."

Olivia's face blanched and she leaned forward with a hand to her chest upon hearing his words. Many of the refugees gasped, and began coming toward Nestor.

"No!" he shouted, lifting his hand up. "She would not want you all to risk your lives. After all she's fought for. Go! And make good use of your lives."

His impatience was so great that his parked airship seeming completely out of reach until he was right in front of it. Once in the cockpit, he skipped half the checks, not even bothering to strap in before he tore off into the sky, the ground receding to a miniaturized military man's strategy board. His grip tightened around the controls as he pushed the limits of what the ship was capable of doing.

The divergence from his intended goal, within Voltan's visualized neural networks, caused striation of electrical signals in a web of flickering noise. He groaned, the frustration and exhaustion adding another impediment to each roadblock that appeared as he tested configurations of the source neurotransmitter.

He had to strike on a solution where the neurons would accept the neurotransmitter as the same, but would respond to it differently. Not merely on an individual level, either— the net response of the cerebral system had to be changed, but the message transmission itself unhindered. He proceeded empirically in uncharted territory, where nanovolts would mean the difference between enlightenment and insanity, and found that he was discovering just how very little was known about the brain.

Flickering pathways lit up like fireworks that followed a wrinkled space, and Voltan lost himself, shifting into overdrive as he bent over a chair with the hood and gloves. He plowed through the imaginary world until he could smell dendrites and taste serotonin. There was no obvious symmetry or correlation between the alterations in the neurotransmitter and the resulting pattern in the brain, but he began picking up on clues, only vaguely aware of Prokhor's annoying interventions to feed him through a straw underneath the hood, in order to ensure he didn't work himself to death. Voltan was so engrossed the feeding straw felt like an intrusion from an alien world.

The same nervous centers were triggered at the same time whenever a suggestion was put forth. He could follow the paths along until they branched, slowing and zooming until the dendritic cavern looked like a firefly-filled forest. Here was where the crux was. One goal with dozens of foci. He slammed the intersection with every shape combination he could think of, until finally the message was relayed in a different direction.

Jumping to another intersection, he switched vistas as though jumping through the reach to Gelion. This one was crowded, dense and bright enough to make him squint. The molecule didn't work here, and he furiously altered it once more, making minute adjustments as he converged on the variation that would work in both situations. It was a small grace that time didn't seem to hold sway in the imagined brain construct.

The final configuration was uncertain, tentative glimmers of reactions almost akin to the pattern of accepted suggestion. Voltan wouldn't allow himself to get excited at this point. He was wary of the baseless persuasion of exhaustion and the risk of giving in to false hopes. He squeezed the molecule, reducing steric hindrance in one area and adding it to another, and watched the ripple effect until he achieved a level of skeptical optimism.

Taking off the hood, his heart pounding and the air in his lungs tasting stale, he walked silently over to the main screen. Prokhor, asleep on a nearby bench, stirred and half-awoke as he watched Voltan spin the molecule into position and focus. Voltan turned to him, a very serious expression on his face. "How do we make it?"

Prokhor sat up quickly, blinking as he widened his eyes to force himself to rise. "Are you sure it—"

Voltan nodded.

Prokhor rubbed his eyes, a bit unnerved. He moved to stand up and fell back down again. "Well," he said, his voice hoarse, "you have to convert the structure into biomachine code."

Voltan pointed to a metal box with a thick glass panel on front, and Prokhor nodded. "You have to make sure the base elemental constituents are within the constraints of the system," he explained, and paused to clear his throat. When he resumed, it was in his normal, breathy voice. "The computer will try to find a source substance for each intermediary reaction, but it doesn't usually work for all of them."

Voltan frowned. "So you have to find some reagents manually?"

"Potentially. But, thankfully, the internal repository is vast enough that we rarely have to do any chemistry by hand."

Prokhor helped Voltan break his protein into manageable sections, circling functional group combinations that would be simple to synthesize, and helping him sort through reaction chains for the difficult parts. The final assembly was the trickiest step, and Prokhor explained that it would also take the longest. After an hour of planning, Voltan hit start and the machine's thermal oven turned on.

"Now we wait?"

"We wait."

"There's no way to speed it up?"

"Each reaction is going about as fast as it can go," said Prokhor. "But the problem that you can never get away from is how many side-reactions occur with different byproducts. Sorting through them is a challenging task, with masspecs and centrifuges, but we are fortunate enough not to have to do any of it. Centuries ago people on Earth used to take days, months, weeks to synthesize and isolate the right protein. Growing it would be just as painful. Now we only have to wait a few hours."

Voltan scrunched up his face impatiently. His mind hummed with the buzz of potential progress, thinking along with the biomachine as it worked. The options split in myriad directions, holding him captive in stillness and silence as he followed them. The sound of someone moving helped him disengage.

It was Prokhor, returning from cleaning himself up.

"Can we use the takoshi in the war?" Voltan asked. His gaze locked onto his friend's, intense with hope.

Prokhor approached him and gripped him by both shoulders. "My Lorel master does not want it," he whispered. "But that's the plan, my friend."

Olivia stared at the panoramic view of the dozen or so final passengers moving up the ramps of the Monatese passenger ship. The processing tables were being packed up. One of the ramps had been drawn in. The wind whistled through the trees. All the noises of people had receded into the innards of the massive ship.

She thought of Voltan and Pleo, and closed her eyes. The only way she could justify her departure was to envision a calm after the hurricane of the war on the 'mold' and rebellion against Di Mon, in which it would be quiet enough for Pleo to escape from the propagandist clutches of Kai'til's gang, and maybe for Voltan to have a better chance of belonging on Monitum. *I'm not abandoning you,* she thought. *I will never abandon you.*

The back of Faren's head faced her as she scanned the few remaining people, and she felt a pang of regret. He really was a lovely boy, and although she wasn't sure how she felt — wouldn't allow herself to explore the emotion — she was going to miss him. He had been an anchor of support through the whole mess and she inwardly dreaded the thought of leading the refugees without him.

Swallowing hard, she moved to his side and waited as he wished a woman and her children a safe flight.

"They'll be all right," he said, smiling with a far-off look in his eyes. "They've been through Hell, but they'll be all right."

Olivia stretched and kissed him softly on the cheek. "I hope we all will."

"We will," he said, turning and wrapping his arms around her.

Olivia's throat felt like she had just gargled a vial of Monatese whisky. "I'll try to come back as soon as I can," she croaked.

Faren looked confused as he pushed his head away from her. "We all will."

She gave him a pained look. "Faren, you can't come onboard. We applied the identification standard to everyone else— only altered people and their children, not even unaltered mothers or father. To make an exception, for you, would slap them in the face."

He sandwiched her hand between his, and smiled. "I'm not an exception, Olivia."

Olivia's heart stuttered. "What are you talking about?" she asked, her voice deadpan.

His gazed wandered around to ensure no one was within earshot. "I got the injection," he said, rolling up his sleeve to expose evidence of a puncture in his forearm.

Olivia felt a tremor of concern that quickly hardened as her shoulders tensed. "What?"

"I knew they wouldn't let me onboard unless I was a genuine refugee," he explained, his smile diminishing as worry creased his face. Frowning at Olivia's silence, he added, "I did it to be with you."

"How!" she exclaimed, refusing to believe it possible.

He gave a tiny shrug, and half-mumbled, "Di Mon's people confiscated some contraband. I... sort of stole a dose."

"Are you crazy?" she said, her lips trembling. "After all we've been through, all we've seen— you want to put your children through the same?"

"We both know that it won't matter," he said, face flushing. "People will hate if they find a reason to. Nothing I do now can ever protect my children from that."

"You can give them a fighting chance, at least!" Olivia threw up her arms and shoved Faren away. "Gods, we're going to need more people on the ground. Monitum needs more clear-minded citizens, and you go and taint yourself to abandon this planet to the likes of Kai'til!"

Faren's face twisted as though she had slapped him. "I'm not abandoning it, and neither are you, right?"

"No," she said, "but I don't have a choice."

"You always have a choice," Faren snapped, his voice rising. "You could stay behind and none of the maniacal idiots would be the wiser. No one's forcing you to go on that ship, Olivia, but I don't think you're going to leave the refugees at a time when they need you most."

Olivia's nostrils flared as she turned away, looking at the clouds sliding past the sun. "Why," she whispered. "You could have led a life without complications."

Faren moved closer to her, lifting his hand tentatively to her shoulder. "If it's complicated, but it's with you, then it's worth it."

Olivia looked into his eyes, feeling suddenly very naked in the wide field. She wanted to tell him to stay behind, to avoid the fate that she knew in her heart would envelop the ship and everyone in it. She wondered if she was cynical for not believing that by fleeing they could leave their troubles behind, but she had a feeling her sick dread would not abate until Kai'til and all of his followers had joined the Watching Dead and were only known through stories. The icy words that would strip Faren of his ignorance and force him to stay behind were on the tip of her tongue, but her anger wouldn't take her there. Instead, anger fizzled into darkness like one of the many reading lamps she and Voltan would go through during their late night slumber parties which had been more like study sessions. She felt tears in her eyes, her vision blurring as she wrapped her arms around Faren. "Fine," she whispered, her voice ragged, "you can come."

She fell into him, her knees quaking as rivulets flowed down her dirty and sallow cheeks. This may be the last time she would see Monitum's green hills and forests, the fields that stretched and opened the horizon until her imagination took care of the rest. There were too many things that she feared to lose in the next instant, all from the sharp lessons learned in the short time since the death of her parents, and so she lost herself in the sensations of Faren's cheek against her hair, the soft grip of his hands, and the smell of sweat and trees.

A few minutes later, Faren helped her wipe her eyes and, holding her hand, they boarded the ship.

Neither Olivia, nor Faren, nor the few remaining Monatese guards noticed Pleo and eight other children sneak up the aft loading ladder that extended alongside the rear landing gear. Pleo punched in the code to retract the ladder and close the door, and smirked. Whether the happy glow that he felt was because he would be able to save his sister, or due to the sheer triumph he felt over outsmarting Liege Monitum's finest, he couldn't tell. "I told you," he whispered in the dark cargo area, "no one knows the ships better than I do."

Chapter 16

Nestor sprinted through the empty streets near the spaceport. The few guards he'd encountered on the street had been easily dispatched, which worried him all the more— it meant most of them were massing near the arena. He had to fight to pace himself, as fury, fear and exertion primed his body for action with a ferocity beyond where he could function and think as a whole person. His boots smacked the rubble-strewn ground as the auditorium came into view.

The open space around it was empty, and only the creaks and moans of the city could be heard above the wind. Nestor slowed, keeping to the shadows as he approached, and scanning the windows of surrounding buildings for any sign of Kai'til's men. Over the nervecloth attached to his ear, the message to assemble was being replayed over and over again. Was it possible Kai'til was having trouble mustering an audience? Nestor was an hour early, but he thought there might be more die-hards who would gather for the best seats.

The back entrance was open, and Nestor crept in past glass-paneled doors and through hallways carved with figures of Earthly gods of Greece, Rome, and India. There were torn posters of some of the plays and shows that had been enacted here before it had become a stage for slaughter.

His breathing frantic, Nestor trembled as he tried to keep his exhalations from announcing his presence. He turned a corner and peered into the auditorium. A mere handful of people were sitting in the audience. There were two guards onstage, holding a tied woman with a potato sack over her head, dressed in shaggy rags.

Remei, he thought. It wasn't going to be easy, but it was certainly better than the full house of bloodthirsty purists that Nestor had expected. He moved through the staircase to the upper level, and crept over to the seats nearest the stage, on a platform that jutted out to allow the richest patrons to feel they were part of the show.

Hold on, my love, he thought. *We'll get out of here together.* Waiting until most of the few audience members had either looked away or closed their eyes, he backed away from the edge in a crouch. A moment later, he exploded toward the railing, one foot planted on the curved gold-colored metal, before he propelled himself toward center stage. He drew his sword and landed right next to the guards, shouts and cries of surprise erupting all around him.

He slashed one of the guards across the throat, and turned just in time to jump away from the other's blade. The audience members were scrambling through the seats toward the stage, and there were only precious seconds before Nestor was outnumbered and surrounded. He grabbed the other guard's sword tip with his bare hand, and yanked the man toward him as the blade sliced his palm. With his other hand, Nestor slashed twice across the guard's vest, huge dark red gashes opening before he kicked the man down.

He slashed the ropes binding Remei's ankles, then began sawing at the ones on her wrists. A furious, stocky man was pulling himself onstage as Nestor severed the cords, and Remei pulled off her hood.

It wasn't Remei.

"Why thank you, my dashing prince," the dark-haired woman said in a mockingly high voice. In the precious instant that shock froze Nestor, she pulled a dagger out of her rags and lunged toward him.

The blade caught Nestor in the shoulder of his sword-arm, and he cried out. The stinging pain sharpened his focus. He grabbed the woman's arm and twisted as he kicked her hard between the legs. She grunted and her cheeks puffed up as the wind was knocked out of her. She released the dagger and Nestor stumbled back as Kai'til's forces surged toward him. In his peripheral vision Nestor could see more troops pouring in through the auditorium entrances.

Through the nervecloth in his ear, he could hear a man laughing. "Triumph, my brothers and sisters! We have found the weeds that prevent us from uniting, and we will cut them down before marching for the future of Monitum."

Nestor felt his throat constrict as he fled backstage. He knew that even if he managed to get outside, Kai'til's forces would have surrounded the building. *Where are you, Remei?* he thought, wincing as he tried to lift his sword arm.

Voltan held the vial before Tideripper, the takoshi, moving it to keep it in front of the lizard as Tideripper darted around, trying to keep its nose away from the synthetic protein. Within a few minutes, however, the takoshi stopped fighting, and Prokhor clapped his hands together.

"Yes!" he cried, crouching down to get a closer look. "Docility is the first sign things are working. Now comes the suggestion."

Prokhor stepped away, opened a drawer in the lab table and pulled out a thick metallic disc with a strap that he slipped over his shoulder. He flicked a switch and the disc began to whir. The side closest to him became transparent, revealing a shiny, spinning liquid inside. Prokhor touched the surface with his fingertip, and a melodious ring echoed through the room, making the takoshi perk up. Voltan could see that the liquid's surface had flexed inwards at the radial point of contact with Prokhor's finger, making a concave depression that breathed like a diaphragm.

Prokhor expertly strummed his fingers over the surface, the spinning liquid responding to his strokes as it flexed and dilated to create a warbling arpeggio intermingled with sharp staccato jolts where he slapped the center and caused the liquid to flatten once more.

The takoshi's head followed the movement of the instrument, until Prokhor started playing a repetitive thrum of bass notes setting up a cadence beneath ringing harmonics.

Voltan felt his fingers tingle at the music, and had to shake his head to regain focus on the large-clawed lizard. The takoshi's head jerked forward and it began to march, its legs barely coordinated, in robotic movements, as it walked headlong toward the edge of the table.

Voltan, too entranced to realize what was occurring, dove at the last moment for the edge and caught the takoshi in his arms as it toppled over. As Prokhor continued playing, the takoshi's legs kept moving.

"Excellent!" said Prokhor, letting the strapped instrument rest against his side when he stopped. "The eliox speaks to the takoshi in ways we can never hope to." He looked on admiringly as the spinning liquid of the instrument slowed to a stop. "And it works." He grabbed both of Voltan's shoulders and shook him a few times. "It works!"

Voltan managed a smile, somewhat ill at ease after Tideripper nearly killed himself. Prokhor's right arm had looked eerily natural playing the eliox, which was about the only time it ever had. Now Prokhor touched him with the same arm and its uncanny nature made him want to shiver. He managed to resist the urge.

They ran a few other tests, making the takoshi jump, roll, and dance all by playing different songs on the eliox. Prokhor's excitement became palpable every so often when his hands shook. When he was satisfied it was working, he took off the strap and set down the eliox.

"What now?" Voltan asked, picking up Tideripper in his arms and petting him.

Prokhor's gaze shifted to an imaginary place in the middle of the wall. "We take to the skies, my friend." He looked down at the takoshi. "I suspect the Lorels are going to try to use takoshi of their own against the refugee passenger ship, and we have to get on and stop them." He turned to the machine. "We need to make more of the protein, right now."

Voltan's heart raced as he thought of his sister and all the others onboard the passenger ship. Although they had left without him, he would still protect and save them. Maybe after all was said and done they'd all appreciate him more, and pay him more attention.

After Prokhor left the room to make the final preparations for their departure, Voltan tapped the screen and started the batch-processing of more of the protein. He listened to the hum of centrifuges and the occasional crack of masspecs as the machine went to work.

Remei awoke with a piece of hay scratching her eyelid, and could feel the indentations the grain had made on her face. Her throat felt dry and hoarse, and she swallowed painfully, avoiding the urge to groan. She heard the outside door slam and people arguing in the hallway outside the hay storage room. Her shoulder ached from the awkward way she had been leaning against the wall while she slept.

"Your Grace, Paxasa doesn't like being interrupted when he's in the middle of a recitation!"

"Hold your tongue before I cut it out," snapped a biting, slightly high-pitched voice that Remei guessed belonged to Kai'til. "We need to redirect the troops now."

Remei wondered if Kai'til had already made his announcement. Had she slept through the whole thing? She twisted amongst the bales of hay, wincing at every small noise she made. Thankfully, the people outside were boisterous enough not to notice as she crept around the hay toward the door. She caught a glimpse of Kai'til's tall yet hunched form as he bobbed toward the spiral staircase at the end of the hall. The protesting guard walked clumsily after him, in a serious dilemma over the well-being of his tongue.

Closing her eyes and taking a deep breath, Remei pulled a dagger out of her cloak. The hilt was warmer on one side than the other, the lumpy metal feeling like a spine between her fingers. She rolled it around until it felt comfortable, then followed the men up the stairs.

Remei crouched near the top. She watched Kai'til shove the guard posted outside the broadcast room, who then fell to the floor. He didn't get up. Paxasa stormed out of the room into the portion of the hallway where it widened.

"Kai'til, what do you think you're—"

Kai'til planted his foot on his Paxasa's chest and kicked him down. "You have forgotten your place," he spat. "I told you to redirect the troops an hour ago, and you keep up with your preachy dogma."

"They need their sermons once a week," Paxasa said, from the floor, on his back. There was anger on his face even though he shuffled away from Kai'til on his elbows. "It maintains constancy for an otherwise chaotic time. You need the balance, Kai'til."

"I need those disgusting traitors dead." Kai'til never stopped moving as he spoke, bobbing back and forth and up and down as though stillness might be bad for his health. "And I have a mob out there who needs to know where to go."

"Why don't you just tell them in person?" snarled Paxasa. He pulled out a pistol and pointed it at the rebel Sheriff of Grianach.

Kai'til made no reply, but hunched forward and stalked closer to the master of propaganda. Remei didn't think there would be a better opportunity, so she crept forward, mere meters separating her and Kai'til.

"Give me your broadcasting codes," Kai'til said quietly. He extended a hand toward Paxasa, who now had his back against the wall at the end of the hallway. "Please, Paxasa. I know your heart is in the right place."

Remei readied the blade in her hand as she moved.

Paxasa swallowed, and looked askance. "They're in the office," he said. "I'll show you where."

Remei could practically feel Kai'til's smile as his hunched form straightened slightly. "All right. Put the gun down, and let us talk over the language of my announcement. You have better words than I."

The compliment went over well. Paxasa accepted Kai'til's offered hand and stood up. He had lowered his gun when Remei lunged forward, knife raised high.

"Watch out!" shouted Paxasa, shoving Kai'til out of the way, his pistol involuntarily firing into the ground as Remei toppled into them. She stabbed Paxasa's arm and he dropped the gun. A moment later Kai'til backhanded her and she felt as though she flew through the air before her head collided with the wall. The world spun and the skin on her face throbbed.

She couldn't see exactly how it happened, but a moment later Paxasa's throat was slit, and he had fallen to the ground, holding his neck as he gurgled blood onto the hard metal floor.

"I have to thank you, lovely," said Kai'til, tearing off the hood of her cloak. "Paxasa here may have been an issue for me, if I was blamed for his death. Your attack is the perfect cover."

She closed her knees together and padded the ground for the dagger, which had slipped out of her hands during her fall. "You needed his codes," she said, her voice sounding hoarse.

"Not really," said Kai'til. "Part of being a good leader is giving the illusion of power to your subordinates. I threatened to take it away from him to make him think he still had something to lose. If he knew he had nothing to hold over my head, he would have shot me right away."

The cold logic mingled with blunt cruelty sent shivers up her spine, and she pushed away from him, wondering if he would do the same or worse to her.

"The hardest part about working around filth," Kai'til mused, glancing aside at Paxasa where he lay unmoving in a pool of his own blood, "is that you can never trust them. They will do what others won't, but they are like caged animals set loose in the wild. He would have shot me just as easily as he does his hourly broadcasts." He sighed.

Remei said nothing, staring at him and not daring to provoke him.

"I'm not going to kill you," he said, as though reading her mind. His mouth moved so exaggeratedly that his nose twitched. He grabbed Remei by the arm. "You are much too pretty to waste."

She gave a wordless cry as Kai'til hauled her to her feet.

"Where's my son?" she shouted, glaring at him as her fate seemed locked in place. "Or do you do the same thing with children as you do with women?"

Kai'til laughed and twisted her away from him, pushing her toward the broadcast room. "You think I have no principles, do you? Well, my dear, children are far too easy and you seem like you'll have a fair amount of fight in you." He flung her to the ground in the mess of cables and recording equipment. "Tell you what," he went on, "if you tell me your boy's name I'll make sure he can watch."

"Go dunk yourself, rat," Remei said, spitting on his shoes.

Kai'til tilted his head to the side before he kicked her hard in the face.

Nestor stumbled as he pushed his way out the back entrance of the auditorium, grunting as his wounded leg burned. To his left, he could see the mob of Kai'til's followers clustering around the entrance, who had somehow missed the possibility of their prey emerging from any other door. Nestor thanked the gods that mob mania wasn't overly intelligent.

It didn't take long for someone to point and shout in Nestor's direction as he sprinted off across the huge open space surrounding the auditorium. Each gunshot made Nestor flinch and run faster, the pain creeping through his muscles although he was able to ignore it. Some of Kai'til's men still hesitated to use forbidden weapons, and even the enthusiasts were untrained in their use. They were terrible shots. At one point a cry of shock suggested an accident, and turmoil broke out with some gang members turning on the culprit. But the majority kept after Nestor.

The angry cries were dissonant with the sounds of Nestor's croaky breaths. Monitum slid beneath pounding feet as slivers of light danced through the clouds, making striped markers of how far Nestor had to go to reach safety. He ran until the aches of his body were mere whispers in the back of his mind.

Through abandoned buildings, across makeshift planks atop buildings that, only a month prior had been in full economic bloom. Now the detritus of destruction had wrapped itself around city life, and a vastly outnumbered Nestor wove through the remains like an Earthworm in a cemetery.

His ears hurt, his pulse an audible throb as he huddled in a dark, rat-infested corner of a shop. His breaths came in stuttering gasps as his diaphragm contracted hard, wanting more air, but he forced it to slow down to keep quiet. The chanting outside grew increasingly faint. He closed his eyes until silence washed over him like rain on a forest fire.

Kicking a rat off him just as it readied to take a chunk out of his ankle, Nestor pushed himself up wearily. If they had lured him in by pretending to have Remei, did that mean they had captured her? Or was she still out there, searching for the children and ready to stop at nothing until she found them?

There were no answers. Too many questions, and not enough time in this life or the next to come to any sort of reconciliation with the madness and insanity that kept cycles ahead of everything else. Nestor's eyes felt heavy as he walked outside, exhausted but robotically checking for danger. He wasn't sure how he would react if more of Kai'til's people found him. Perhaps he would keep running, keep fighting, but for how long he couldn't bear to think.

The roads were quiet on the path to the spaceport, and there were almost no guards when he got there. It was a stark contrast to the hum of activity when he'd arrived. *Is this the prosperity you promised, Kai'til?* he thought, glancing back at the gray, sallow state of the city before he ducked into the empty spaceport halls.

Out of habit, he moved carefully and quietly, the silence more unnerving than the chaos. He was a few berths away from his ship when he heard murmurs tremble through the stale air. Freezing, he stalked along the wall until he found the room from which the voices were coming. A sick feeling of recognition made his skin tingle, sprinkled with goose bumps.

"They are preparing to launch as we speak," said a breathy male voice. Nestor felt the blood drain from his face as he recognized the speaker, the man who had kidnapped his son years ago and was a master of behind-the-scenes manipulation: the Caddy. He took his name after an Old Earth sport where there was someone who handed the players the right tools, but never participated in the game himself.

"Good," said a woman's voice. It sounded ordinary and mild. "You went too far when you gave them Lorel-like genius, Prokhor. The intent was to shepherd the Sevolites and maintain their fear of science, but you introduced a whole new set of problems. Sigmund wanted the Ald'erdas' work dishonored, not all Monitum at risk of a backlash from Fountain Court should too much of what's taken place here be discovered." The woman sounded more like an annoyed Nesak housewife upbraiding a relative for tracking mud into the living room than someone powerful and terrible. But the things she spoke of struck Nestor's tired brain like hits on a challenge floor.

"I've told you before, there is no way to tell some of the side-effects," the Caddy said, defensively.

"Nonsense," the woman told him off in her mild-mannered, parental manner. "Don't feign ignorance. You know better. What were you thinking, Prokhor?"

There was a lengthy pause. "I thought that it would stir up things even more if there was an intelligence boost among those modified."

"Too much of a stir, young man. Sometimes I wonder if you really are half-Lorel, or more Vrellish than your genes might let on."

Nestor edged closer to the door, but didn't dare peer in. He could hear the Caddy suck in an impatient breath. His thoughts threatened to take off and race with the implications of what he was hearing, but the urgency of the moment forced him to listen and leave speculation until later.

"Are we done here, Dartha?" the Caddy asked.

"Are you going to follow orders this time?" she answered sternly.

Nestor imagined how the Caddy must have been on the verge of strangling Dartha, or trying to sear a hole through her skull with his glare.

"Even if I was really here beside you," she said, "I hope you aren't naïve enough to think you could threaten me with violence if you chose to indulge your Vrellish leanings."

What does that mean? Nestor wondered. *How is she communicating with him if she's not here? What terrible force can hold sway over the Caddy?*

"So, to Sanctuary Reach I go, with all of my toys," the Caddy answered her in a sing-song manner.

"They are not your toys, Prokhor," said Dartha, as though this were a topic she had covered before. "They are people. People whose existence you are responsible for. As you are responsible for any backlash or unforeseen complications they cause."

The Caddy's voice sounded like he was speaking to the ground. "Yes, master."

"Once they're rounded up we'll be able to deal with them appropriately," Dartha conjectured, sounding hopeful and not entirely certain.

"Why not just kill them all right now? It will satisfy the populace," said the Caddy. Nestor felt the chill on his skin tingle again.

"I hate this!" was the woman's immediate response, spoken in earnest. There was an awkward pause. "Yes, that might be easiest. Surgical. But the empire Sevolites cannot see our hand. They must think the ship was lost in space, or struck by plague, or any number of things, but the point is that we can't create the illusion with smoke and mirrors while we are so close to the light source. We must get them off Monitum. Away from here. Give Liege Monitum a chance to clean up and protect Monitum from reprisals by Fountain Court."

"So off I go, into the realm of darkness," said the Caddy, with mock gravity.

"Don't be coy. Just get the job done."

Nestor didn't want to be around when the Caddy — and Dartha's mysterious presence, if that was possible — emerged from the room. His heart thudding, he crept away from the door, the argument fading into a faint whisper that haunted his thoughts. When he was out of sight, he gave an involuntary shudder as horror enveloped him. He shook himself, trying to get rid of the dread and fear that had started to make his hands tremble. *I have to get to the ship*, he thought. *I have to stop them from taking off.*

He had never before heard of a living Lorel, but from the way Dartha spoke, that was all she could be. It had been more manageable when he had thought Kai'til was manipulating the situation for his own ends, but the layers of puppetry made Nestor's skin crawl. First the implication that the Caddy had been acting on Lorel orders to tempt the Ald'erdas a step too far in their bio-science revival project with the purposeful intent of having it rebound on them. Then the Caddy — or Prokhor — overstepping his own bounds and being reined in by a Lorel overseer And what, if anything, did Di Mon know about it as Liege Monitum? Did they communicate with him? Or was he, too, a puppet behaving predictably given the right stimulus?

It all made Nestor feel small, a fish out of water far away from any sea. As he made his way to his ship and climbed in, his thoughts drifted to the Lorel device he had found years ago that had allowed him to see anyone's darkest desires through soul touch. His friend, Frean, had exposed himself as a sadistic pirate and they had been put in a situation that only one of them would walk away from.

Nestor felt the same as he had that day, when the illuminating clarity of the truth had revealed a twisted ugly mess that was more sobering and a greater test of his strength than anything else. His hands shook at the controls as he rose up into the air in his envoy-class *rel*-ship. He closed his eyes for a moment and whispered a prayer to the gods.

Chapter 17

There were few green planets in the Gelack Empire, and Olivia and the refugees had been forced to flee one of the universe's greatest treasures. The stretches of fields, the luscious forests and the metal labyrinth of the spaceport in which Olivia had grown up receded into nothing as the Monatese passenger ship pulled out of the atmosphere.

Olivia missed the sight of Monitum when they docked at an orbital station to be transferred to a *rel*-capable freighter. Security was tight but this time solely with respect to keeping whoever came on the shuttle from Grianach from having any interactions with local personnel or residents. It was surprisingly easy to accomplish, since the orbital station was under fleet control. More than once, Olivia feared troops would march in and quietly exterminate them all. Troops without swords, dressed in armor, with weapons designed for occupation duty in lawless places in the empire. After all, it could be argued that by their very existence she and the other refugees from Grianach had dropped the shield of honor. Stepped outside the bounds of *Okal Rel*. Cheated. Let themselves be tainted by Lorel science which made their humanity questionable, or worse— non-existent.

But while they were allowed no contact with anyone on the military station, they were not molested. They were not even searched or questioned or checked against the loading roster, so reluctant did their fleet minders seem to have anything more to do with them than absolutely necessary. Olivia was forced to wonder whether the troops had been told they might carry some kind of contagion. But whatever the reason for hands-off dispatch, they were hustled off their shuttle onto a freighter refitted in anticipation of their arrival to take passengers, in a sub-standard manner, and in less than an hour they were in a new ship, with a military pilot and surrounding Monatese *rel*-fighter escorts, en route to the jump that led to Sanctuary.

Once, in the jostling rush to get everyone transferred, Olivia thought she'd glimpsed Pleo. She'd quickly admonished herself for wishful thinking making her see things, because the boy concerned ignored him when she called his name, and was quickly lost in a sea of faces.

As soon as they were underway, Olivia went around and checked the refugees, making sure they had enough food and water. Her cart was practically empty by the time she made it around, and there were only a few crackers left for her as she pushed it back into the cargo hold. The people had been grateful, giving her the best smiles they could manage under the circumstances. The pain of exile laced every facial expression, and she wondered if the same had happened to her. Maybe with enough time, pretending to be happy would transform into the real thing.

She searched for the bulkhead with the red and blue striped towel that she and Faren had used to mark their spot amongst the cramped families. The air felt stuffy. The gritty feeling of traveling under *rel*-skimming conditions was settling into her bones. They were keeping to one skim-fac. It would take hours.

"Hey you," she said, seeing Faren's form lean in the shadows against a girder— part of the makeshift rigging installed to turn a cargo bay into passenger transport for a thousand people.

"Fancy meeting you here," Faren croaked, his voice raspy and strained.

Olivia felt her features sink as she rushed to his side. "What happened?" she asked, her eyes adjusting to the gloom as she put her hand on his forehead. "You're sweating enough to have a bath."

"Not sure, honey," Faren said, smiling with his eyes half-shut in delirium. He traced a single finger up Olivia's arm, before resting his knuckles against her triceps. "You know you're beautiful, right?"

Olivia frowned, ignoring his question. "Did you eat anything, Faren?"

"Not anything out of the ordinary," he said, closing his eyes and taking a deep breath. There were murmurs from the berths around Olivia and she could sense everyone recoil in fear that they would catch whatever ailed the country boy.

"I'm getting you some water and food," she said, standing up. She turned to the mass of eyes in the shadows who watched her and hushed as she stared back. "Does anyone here have medtech training?"

Most of the refugees looked away, and none came forward. She knew it was too much to hope for.

Some women wearing shawls and travelling gowns offered Faren blankets while Olivia ran off to see what medical provisions were available in the storage lockers. She caught two boys trying to tamper with the lock and snarled at them. "You think you aren't getting enough?"

The boys turned toward her, looking afraid for a moment before they realized they outnumbered her. As their expressions turned menacing, Olivia stepped forward and slapped one after the other, hard. "Shame on you," she said. "You're young and healthy. Has all the pain of Monitum taught you nothing about greed and what's rightfully yours?" She grabbed them by the ears and hauled their heads down to waist level, as the boys yelped. "We do not have time for this, and you boys need to be helping me, not creating more problems for—" Her voice faltered as she thought of Faren, sweating and struggling to breathe in the corner. "—those who need us."

Dragging the boys out of the cargo hold, she let them go and watched them stalk away sheepishly. After she had gotten some allergy medication and some painkillers — all that they had in stock — she returned to Faren with some water and protein. The women who had given him the blankets were crouched beside him, clutching pendants they wore around their necks while they closed their eyes and murmured prayers. She had seen prayers before, but the pendants seemed like something out of a storybook.

Her hands searched the empty place around her neck, where her Old Earth necklace had once hung before all promise had been snatched away. She'd lost it after Faren had pretended it was a bomb, and they'd fled from one struggle into another. She stared at the women as though they had wronged her by keeping what she could not.

"Thank you," she said to the women, hoping they took the cue to give her and Faren some space. They opened their eyes, bowed their heads to her and rose, but didn't go very far away.

Raising an eyebrow, Olivia sat down beside Faren. "Here, drink this," she said, lifting the water to his lips. Faren struggled to tilt his head enough, and Olivia tried not to panic at how quickly his health had deteriorated. "You're going to get better, you hear me?"

Faren grunted his affirmation as he sipped. "Delicious," he breathed after he finished.

"You think you can stomach some food?" Olivia asked, noticing that her hands trembled with the packs of protein.

Faren frowned as she showed him the synthetic high-born food.

"Let's try," she said. "You need the energy."

She spooned the brown paste into his mouth, and his face seemed less and less pale. She felt a tremendous release of pressure in her chest, as though she had been stockpiling a pocket of air for worry. But he'd only been hungry! The ease and simplicity of the situation soothed every part of her, making her skin tingle and her face lighten with a plain smile.

A few minutes passed before he jerked away from her, retching in the cramped space. He groaned as though a serrated knife were being dragged across metal. It was loud enough to echo through the chamber. Olivia shot up and glanced frantically around for anything to offer him. A man came by and offered her a bucket which she gratefully placed beside Faren.

His vomiting became more and more hoarse as his stomach emptied and his body tried to purge an unseen enemy the only way it knew how. Olivia watched as liquid spewed out of him— more than he had drunk.

She tried to reason about what might have gone wrong, what he might have caught, and her mind raced. There was no illness to speak of amongst the refugees — thank the gods — and everyone had been eating the same food. Most of the rations were even split up, so if one was contaminated someone else would have gotten sick. She had been with Faren every waking moment that she could spare, and the only thing he had done differently was.

The injection. She scanned his arms and shoulders, then pawed at his pant legs, pushing them up one after the other until his quadriceps were exposed. About a third of the way up from his right knee was a large red spot, almost purple at the center before it faded out radially in fragmented veins. The crisscrossing blood bursts across his skin looked like red paint splatter. Olivia covered her mouth.

She felt stupid for not realizing it earlier. He was reacting to the injection, and whatever Lorel magic had coursed through her father's veins and brought destruction to the entire region of Grianach was now killing her beloved.

"Father, if you're watching this," she said as tears streamed down her face, "give him the strength of your blood. Give him mine!" Her voice cracked and many people around her turned away, either from embarrassment or because they felt like intruders into Olivia's privacy. "Please," she said, grabbing Faren's hand as his chest heaved, "please."

A crowd of people replaced those who crept away, and began humming a hymn of prayer together around Faren's nook. Again, Olivia saw relics and ornaments that some held out as they prayed, and she couldn't make sense of it. None of the customs she was aware of contained anything of the sort. Some knelt on ornate mats — the only things they had salvaged from their homes — and bowed deep on their knees. It felt like a dream, and she scanned them to gauge their sincerity.

"May the Goddess heal you," said one of the women wearing a shawl, who had given Faren a blanket. She stepped forward and outstretched her hand with her palm overtop the sick young man.

"Which Goddess?" Olivia murmured, pain and worry creasing her features.

"The only Goddess," the woman said, her face serene but laced with conviction. "Our Goddess, who watches everything and sees all."

Olivia's jaw dropped, but she said nothing. As long as they wished the best for Faren, it didn't matter which gods of Old Earth were invoked. *Whoever and whatever,* she thought, *just heal him.*

"He's reacting to the highborn injection," Olivia said, trying to project her voice despite her dry throat. "If any of you can help in any way, please." She turned back to Faren. "He needs everything we can give him." *He deserves it.*

The refugees came forward, each offering a household remedy and benediction of some kind or another. Olivia watched in amazement as a plethora of beliefs were laid bare before her, hidden beneath the surface through their struggles and travels. There were many who now believed in a single goddess or god. Some thought that the only explanation for the allowance of death that had occurred was that there was a war in progress among the Watching Dead, and the decent souls couldn't manage the scale of everything that was occurring, and just did what they could, while vile and selfish ones — those denied rebirth for too long — took desperate measures by whispering to their descendants to violate *Okal Rel* in order to secure them highborn bodies.

Others took alternative stances, believing in single deities from Old Earth, or favored Sevolites among the Watching Dead, that could bring blessing to Faren and restore his health. Demeter, Hera, Apollo, Venus, Athena, past Avas and lieges of Monitum— Olivia saw them all invoked at some point or another. Faren finally stopped vomiting and she caressed his hair while he slept and more people came by. The number of pendants, scrolls and trinkets was astonishing, as so many Monatese had created something sacred out of keepsakes from their homeland. She was wondering which was correct, which of them would help best, when Faren touched her arm.

"Olivia," he whispered, his voice barely audible through the murmurs of surrounding families. "You know, there's so much ugliness that we've seen since your parents… but your beauty and spirit outshines all the bad. The armies of maniacs who hunted us down cannot stand in the sunshine of your soul. You have the blessings of the Watching Dead and nothing is more powerful." His words were slurred and a bit hard to make out.

Olivia put a hand against his hot cheek, wondering if space-sickness was also part of his problem. He was only a Petty Sevolite. Not even a highborn. "You're just babbling," she said.

He traced his finger up and down her forearm, shaking his head slowly— more as if it lolled from one side to the other than a deliberate, controlled motion. "No, I'm not. I'm offended, actually."

Olivia ran her fingers through his hair as tears glistened in her eyes. "Faren, why did you do it?"

He let out a heavy sigh. "You know, of all the decisions I've made that could be classified as dumb, I thought this would be the last on the list."

She could see the loss and resignation in his face as he began tracing his finger on her arm once more. "It's not how I wanted it, but I'm not the only one who can say that." He craned his neck to look at all the refugees and supporters who stood close by. "They're pretty devout, aren't they?"

"Yes, it looks like they're not pulling any punches, creating deities just for you," Olivia said, her face a mixture of agony and humor, "my love."

Faren squeezed her hand.

Olivia tried to give Faren some water once more, but he vomited it up even more quickly than before. His breaths came in sharp gasps and he could hardly speak, so Olivia just sat by his side and held one of his hands, while he traced up and down her forearm with the other.

She whispered to him of their home, telling him how the orchards would be ripening soon, and the succulent fruit ready to fill the hungry stomachs of the children. He murmured and smiled with closed eyes, and Olivia carried on talking about anything that could bring him joy. It took all of her effort not to stand up and scream at the gods, Watching Dead — whatever it was that controlled fate — to spare Faren.

A few among the crowd of onlookers dispersed, but the majority remained seated nearby, whether to convince themselves or Faren and Olivia of the validity of their faith,

Olivia couldn't be sure. She suspected most of them were just doing as she was, in their own way—sending him love.

The rumble and creaks of the ship were the only markers of time in the dayless reaches of space, and Olivia had no idea how long she lay with Faren. He could swallow nothing, and he had begun to soil himself, making the hall smell putrid. She cleaned him as best she was able. The planets turned, moons spun and systems edged along as two pinpricks within the massive empire spent their last moments together. Olivia's mind was in a daze, a mixture of denial and appreciation twisting in a hurricane that she made no attempt to control.

After a while Faren murmured no more, but simply held her hand and continued to slink his finger up and down her arm, resting his knuckles against her forearm. The sensation felt like the final strand and she wanted to grip his finger, to open it up and shout at him not to leave her. But she didn't.

When his finger stopped moving, a shudder rose through her like glass about to shatter at resonance. She gasped as her chest convulsed and she squeezed his hand, putting her other on his forehead. He was cooling despite the sweat on his forehead, and she felt for his pulse. It took her several minutes to steady her hand and accept what she was seeing and feeling.

"No!" she screamed, her voice shaking the frame of the ship. She burst into sobs, her body twitching uncontrollably as an anvil collapsed onto her heart. Between gasps and tears, the women took her away, murmuring soothing words to a girl far beyond their aid.

From the bowels of the cargo hold, Pleo and his child warriors had watched Olivia come back and forth for medical supplies. Most of them were hungry to attack, but he had stayed their hands— the time was not right yet. He knew that Olivia was enslaved by the adults and would not betray them without much persuasion. The adults needed to go first.

Olivia's scream rang through all the way down to the depths and nooks between the crates where Pleo perched uncomfortably. Sigurd watched his face for signs of what their next move would be, his face an expressionless mask.

"Let's move," Pleo whispered, and they all crept out of the shadows like ants from a dirt mound.

The hold door hissed open into the slightly fresher air of the passage leading up, on one side, to crew quarters and through a door, on the other side, to another section of the cargo hold. Even though the air was less stale, Pleo could still smell sweat from the overcrowded berths beyond the door.

"The children will resist," Pleo instructed, just loud enough to be heard. "But they are not to be killed. Our enemies are the adults who brought this upon us, but remember— if a child is willing to fight to the death to protect evil, do what you must."

"Are the others close behind us, you think?" Sigurd asked, his voice level.

Pleo imagined Enid — who had resisted his command the most of anyone — leading the charge in space to protect them against the inevitable attack of Kai'til's men, using the envoy ships they'd stolen.

"We can trust them to do their duty," Pleo said. "They'll wipe out anyone who might try to kill us in a shake-up."

He could see the threads of worry sewn amongst the children's faces. "They will succeed," he said, the words coming out almost like an order to toughen up.

There was a stairwell leading up to where an earlier reconnoitering mission had taught Pleo to expect the most competent adults to be gathered in the crew quarters like an impromptu council receiving word from others about conditions on the cargo floor. Voices could be heard above, and the children readied their weapons— some with swords, others with guns.

Tired of running, most of the people would be too exhausted to fight. That's what Pleo hoped.

Peeking over the last step, the children could see a pair of men coming toward them, and they scrambled off, silently moving underneath until the echoes of boots above them gave the signal to attack. Wrapping their hands around the ankles of the men, the children yanked, and the men toppled down the stairs, crying out asynchronously with the smacks of their bodies against each step.

The children pounced on the men, drowning out their cries amidst the *slurp-thumps* of repeated stabbings. The children gazed at one another, the fire in their eyes a palpable emotion.

Waving them up, Pleo could see more people coming down the hallway, asking one another if they had being hearing things. He signaled the children to get ready.

There were three men and two women. A man and a woman came down the stairs first, and gasped as they saw the mutilated remains of their friends. An instant later they were tripped and hauled into the trap.

Pleo and Sigurd dashed up and slashed at the feet of two of the three remaining self-appointed adult leaders of the refugees, and their enemies barely had a chance to draw their swords before they fell to the ground. Tearing his sword violently across the side of one man's neck, Pleo watched an unarmed woman scream and run away. *So much for supporting the group,* he thought as he began to give chase. She had almost arrived at the door to the converted cargo hold, where she could warn everyone.

Pulling out his gun, Pleo steadied the pistol in his hands, took aim and fired. The bullet caught the woman in the shoulder— much too high. She staggered, but kept running. By the time Pleo fired a second time, she had gotten through the door.

His mind raced. "Regroup!" he shouted. "Now your training is going to be more important than ever." The blood-stained clothing of the children who joined him had a few tatters, but most had been unharmed. Some of the junior ones were shaking after their first kills.

Then, without warning, the whole freighter gave a shudder that wasn't quite physical and a klaxon sounded, belatedly, notifying those on board they were about to drop out of skim.

Chapter 18

Voltan's mind felt spread too far as he and Prokhor matched velocity with the refugees' ship and slid into a dock that closed over their envoy-class ship. He had never been in space before, despite all the time he had spent around the dock. Images of the interior and inner workings of the crafts flitted through his thoughts, and his stomach surged as they ceased deceleration and the perception of gravity lightened. The stars were brighter than he had ever seen, and seemed both tantalizingly close and far away, an optical illusion that wouldn't sort itself out no matter how hard he stared at it. He had intended to keep track of Monitum on Prokhor's nerve-cloth display of the stars as an emotional anchor to which he could orient and find stability, but the swirling mass of bright specs seized upon his pattern-matching genius with demands for resolution that exhausted him until he closed his eyes and settled into thinking, instead, about proteins.

It took all his concentration to keep from retching as Prokhor brought the *rel*-skimmer to a nice halt, and the freighter that had swallowed them transitioned to *rel*-skimming once more, restoring the sense of gravity. He swallowed a few times to try and quell the sick feeling in his stomach as Prokhor unstrapped and went to the back to grab the tank of protein they had brought with them. The caged takoshis skittered as he walked by them, just as shell-shocked as Voltan after the flight.

"Come on," Prokhor said sharply, beckoning him up. "We need to move quickly."

Voltan unstrapped and felt a surge of adrenaline hit him as he imagined the Lorels laying schemes to out-think him and Prokhor. *Olivia, I'm coming for you,* he thought. *Don't worry. Everything will be all right soon.*

Grabbing the takoshis and cooing at them to behave themselves, Voltan sucked in a breath as Prokhor opened the skimmer hatch. The hiss of pressure equalization ushered in a metal cavern with lights brighter than any of the stars on their way here. As his eyes adjusted Voltan saw Prokhor already moving down the ramp, his strange arm swinging awkwardly as he propped the tank on his opposite shoulder. There was no one else in the area, and Prokhor moved as though he already knew the ship's layout.

His footsteps feeling strange and his ears straining to recalibrate themselves, Voltan followed. The takoshis jiggled around in their cages as he jogged to catch up, the high bulkhead arches emphasizing the lofty ceiling above them. Prokhor stood by the exit from the docks, and as Voltan caught up he could hear shouting.

"We could be too late," Prokhor muttered, frowning at the tank. "There's no time left, Voltan."

Voltan's vision sharpened as his heart thudded. They slinked out into the hallway and Prokhor opened a locked service door that led via a ladder down to some of the drive and system chambers. Clambering down, Voltan balanced the cages between his chest and the ladder.

"Shhh," he whispered. The takoshis were more and more frightened as they curled up into trembling balls, trying to find a safe posture. "It'll be okay, I promise."

A few rings from below made the takoshis suddenly stiffen and stop making noise. They fell from one side to another as Voltan nearly dropped them on the last few ladder rungs. Prokhor caught the cage, his eliox strapped over his shoulder. The liquid inside still rippled with the last few notes he had played. Prokhor's face was sober.

The noisy room had tubes and nervecloth interfaces all over, and Voltan instinctively began working out what it was all for, while Prokhor headed to a section with many valves and gas fittings. He tapped the nervecloth display and Voltan realized what he was doing: opening up the air supply.

Voltan limped over with the cage of takoshis on his hip. "Do we need to do that? We have all the takoshis right here."

Prokhor didn't look up. "The Lorels have their own takoshis, and we must be sure they don't turn against us."

Voltan couldn't help picturing the hordes of refugees who would also be inhaling an aerosol form of the protein he had discovered. Including his sister. He felt a cold vine twist around him as he realized some of the dreadful implications. "Are you sure that it's safe for Sevolites to inhale?" he asked, eyes locked on his mentor as the Lor'Vrel connected a hose to the protein tank.

Prokhor paused, then looked up with a smile. "Don't worry, my friend. It won't hurt anyone." He turned the valve, and the tank gave a whisper as the protein aerosol fed into the ventilation system.

Nestor sailed over the trees with a tight grip on the controls of his envoy ship. He was flying lower and faster than he should, as he tried to reprocess his feelings about the Monatese who had been trying to kill him for so long. He wasn't sure if he could blame Kai'til or his followers anymore, armed with the knowledge that Prokhor, the Caddy, had been guiding it all with a twisted hand.

He reached the empty field where the passenger ship had been loaded, and immediately pulled up and away. He was barely out of the atmosphere before he started cat-clawing his way out toward the jump point for the Sanctuary Reach.

It was no surprise when ward ships buzzed by him but it took only a moment to drop out of skim and reassure them of his identity. It was no good asking for help, though. Not when he was engaged on business Liege Monitum was trying to prevent the rest of Monitum, and the empire, ever knowing about.

Nestor started *rel*-skimming at four skim'facs, his *grip* wobbling as his rage and concern distracted him from flying. Getting to the jump to Sanctuary was painful and he could feel the tension pulse through his body as he pushed himself to the limit of his tired state. He gasped as he pulled back to a skim'fac to avoid alarming ward ships that came out to greet him from the Sanctuary Station, and braced for zero-g when he dropped out of skim to communicate.

The station authorities acknowledged his identity and the proofs of welcome Di Mon had provided Nestor. To his dismay, the authorities told him no unscheduled freighter had arrived ahead of him, to pass through the jump to Sanctuary Reach. Nestor thanked them and waited, watching traffic come and go as he wracked his brain for any technique the Caddy might have been using to hide.

Unless he doesn't intend them to get this far, Nestor thought, recalling the conversation with Dartha Lorel.

Nestor floated in order to get some reprieve from flying, the weightlessness nevertheless making his head ache and stomach twist. The hours ticked by as he switched between cat-clawing and floating in order to try and stay awake.

As the wait stretched out, Nestor grew uneasy and wondered if he was starting to get space-drunk from the high adrenal exertion he was forcing on his body. It took several minutes for him to think of where else the Caddy might have gone.

Of course. The Caddy was the one handing out the tools, not the man to be dealt orders. If told to go to Sanctuary, he would do the exact opposite. And the opposite of out-of-the-way Sanctuary... was Gelion. The heart of everything, the place Di Mon was hell-bent on preventing from learning about the scandal in Grianach District, and the area where the most damage and chaos would be incurred by the Caddy's playthings.

Nestor shot away from the jump to Sanctuary as fast as he could, his wake rocking some ships that had just dropped out of skim as he surged past. He pushed to seven skim'facs and could feel his skin tingle. Whether from the blood dripping down his nose or the threat of losing his *grip*, he couldn't tell. He ate space.

A good fifteen minutes from the heavily guarded jump to Gelion, he spotted the signs of a shake-up ahead and made for it. He barely avoided becoming space debris as he passed through an arc of dust that was most likely all that remained of a shattered ship.

His *nervecloth* display was assaulted with so much activity he could hardly differentiate between ships. He could feel the soul touch of so many pilots around him he had trouble breathing. Two dots flitted off the display as the pilots were dunked— he had no idea which side they were on.

He fell into wake-lock with the closest ships, and could immediately feel that they were loyal to Di Mon and not Kai'til. He let the pilot's *grip* extend over him enough to share a wordless purpose: *Yes, friend, we want the same thing.* The message was powerful enough to get the pilot to back off and Nestor fell into formation with Di Mon's forces.

Where's Di Mon? thought Nestor, swinging out and around at a dangerous three skim'facs. There were far too many ships to be rel-skimming this close together, much less this close to the jump to the empire's capitol.

A recklessly angry pilot dropped out of nowhere onto Nestor and the other Monatese fighters. Nestor's chest wrenched as the wake threatened to tear him and his ship apart. He struggled with the controls as his vision blurred, but maintained enough *grip* to keep flying. The Monatese fighters beside him weren't so lucky, and they dropped into gap, dunked and time-slipping.

He could feel the heavy soul-touch of the enemy pilot as he made a second pass to finish Nestor off. A raw, harsh fury with little other complexity came screaming at him, and he pushed away, slamming down to half a skim'fac before flipping and going the opposite direction. He had to avoid several ships on the way back, but those were nothing compared to the unadulterated hatred. Against that emotion there was no bartering, no squeezing between the unconscious spaces in the way that he normally used to overpower weaker pilots. This wasn't a strong pilot in all dimensions, but just one of such singularity that the shell couldn't be cracked.

He rocked through the wakes of a formation of five ships, and suspected them to be ward ships from the jump vicinity, attracted by the shake-up. Trying to shimmer a peaceful signal toward them as they fell back and surrounded him, he knew they wouldn't be able to tell friend from foe. The landscape was replete with ships that had no business there, and they had no reason to discriminate. He pulled away gracefully, hoping they would take the hint that he wasn't running from them.

Amongst the scattered patches of dots on his *nervecloth* Nestor saw a larger one that remained solid and relatively stable throughout his orbits around the nexus of the fighting. *The passenger ship*, he thought, a mixture of fear and relief at having guessed the Caddy's plan. *I'm not too late.*

He tried to classify the dots as either defending or attacking the ship, and moved in on the ones attacking. The emotion he felt as he approached was simple and easy to unmask: the veil of righteousness and hypocrisy of someone who wanted more than life had dealt out. The reasons overlain were superficial and pointless in soul-touch, and Nestor dunked two pilots as he flexed his will proclaiming everything he believed to be right: the innocent lives of everyone who had suffered, his son, his wife, all with a certainty lacking any pause.

Rolling his *rel*-fighter in the direction over his shoulder in a wide trajectory, he surged toward the group of enmeshed fighters that pushed back and forth against one another nearest the passenger ship. Their wakes sent shock waves through *rel*-space, and Nestor was assaulted by yells inside his skull as the soul-touch became a soul-slap from the sheer number of colliding wills.

Dropping into the fray, he nearly lost control as the ripples rocked him back and forth. He thought of Remei and of Enid who formed pillars in his mind, and he maintained course on the outer edge of the cluster.

Then the sensation hit him. The raw anger and self-righteousness that could not be punctured, the twisted emotional armor that he never would have thought possible. There was but a faint glimmer of the human being behind the monster that controlled the ship, and if it weren't so familiar Nestor would not have noticed it at all.

The quiet curiosity, the firm resolve and stubborn devotion to Cam were fine trembles on the shell's membrane that Nestor could not put into words. He knew, though, as his will shrank against the encroaching rage, that it was Enid.

A tremendous sense of loss and pain came over Nestor, fueled and cascading with the anger his son directed at him and everyone else. If it weren't for something inside, the thing which made every father stand up when everything else had fallen, Nestor would have been crushed and dunked then and there.

Stripped of all the carefully-honed outer defenses through his years in the Nesak war and countless skirmishes thereafter, all that remained of Nestor's *grip* was his love for Enid and the refusal to acknowledge that the sickening presence that compressed him was his son.

The other children, just as angry as Enid, surrounded Nestor. He could barely feel them, however, and anyone else's presence made no difference to the pure bond between father and son. A tendril connected them, no matter how much Enid tried to hate, and it was that which kept Nestor alive.

Their wake grew so large any other ships broke off, unable to contend with the torrential catastrophe that seemed inevitable as space ripped and crashed under the shearing clutch on the edge of reality.

Whether the decision was conscious or not, Nestor would never know. His belief in his son's capacity became a tangible presence, growing and ebbing amidst the turmoil. Soon it was clear that the hatred was irreconcilable, that something had to diminish in order to allow space for something else to blossom. The choice about which path to take, what to sacrifice, was hardly a choice at all, for the only tendril which had dragged him this far now contradicted its own existence.

Nestor let go, his soul winking into a dot before a cascade of energy surged outward in an explosive wave. Enid's emotional carapace cracked to let in a sliver of that energy, which was enough for the entire message to be felt.

I love you, son, no matter what.

Enid, a child alone in the aftermath of the chaos, trembled as he gasped for air, his chest convulsing. His uncontrolled envoy ship drifted at high velocity but was practically stationary compared to the other *rel*-skimmers. He floated in his straps, feeling vomit rise into his throat. Everything seemed very alien and far away, the vastness too much to comprehend as the stars twinkled in weightless wonder. As he rotated slowly, his eyes flitted over the controls of his *rel*-ship. He swallowed and squeezed his eyes shut. Tears clustered into spherical globes that drifted away under limited gravity just as quickly as everything he had held dear.

The skitter of claws against metal shook him and he turned to see Cam the takoshi trying vainly to gain footing in a world with little gravity. Loosening his straps, the pain seemed to lessen as he took the bizarre creature in his hands. The familiarity calmed his breaths, and when Cam swatted at the tear globules, Enid let a small smile cross his lips.

Father, he thought, frowning at the muddled impressions flitting through his mind. *Mother,* he realized with a gasp, the urgency gripping him as quickly as the panic had let go.

"Okay, Cam," he said with a croaking voice. "We *grip* together, and go together."

Enid didn't wait to see if the takoshi understood. He boosted into skim again and away from the jump to Gelion, and toward Monitum. Where the knowledge of Remei's whereabouts had come from, he couldn't explain. An intuition coalesced out of the intense sharing he'd just experienced in his blind rage? A message from the Watching Dead? It was impossible to tell. But the why, he definitely understood.

Chapter 19

The light brightened then dimmed in the main passenger area, the ship's automatic responses overriding the refugees' wish for sleep. Olivia felt as though the slow ebbing marked the trickling away of a pointless and ever-losing battle. She stared off into space as the voices of various religious devotees drifted around her as though their volume was controlled by the light. She had thought — almost hoped — that if Faren died, she would go into a clear dream that would at least take her away from reality. The curse that usually plagued her when she least expected it didn't make an appearance, however.

Part of her wanted to go back to the berth she'd shared with Faren and pretend, for as long as she could, that he was still there. Most of all, she wanted the senseless struggle and pain to end. Her glassy eyes filled and spilt over tears that became the only external indication she was alive.

"May God be with you," said a man, passing by in a Monatese robe he had modified into what he must have deemed religious garb. He closed his eyes and raised his hand in blessing as he passed by each passenger and repeated the same thing.

"You say it as though there is only one and he isn't mad!" snapped one woman, batting his hand away as she stood. "Don't involve me in your heathen betrayal of *Okal Rel*. If I pray, I will pray to my ancestors."

The man stopped and smiled beatifically. "The only ones who have betrayed *Okal Rel* are those who have hunted us down." His posture was an irritating mixture of pretense and phlegmatism.

The woman shoved him away. "Stop it. You act like a few kind words can make up for what's happened, and what continues to happen. If you were any more naive and vacuous the ship would implode."

The man's smile flickered on his face before he bowed and tried to move off. He didn't get far, however, before someone else stood and joined in. "Don't attack him. He's just trying to spread some of our meager supply of good cheer."

"He's forcing his twisted beliefs on us to try to mask the truth."

"What would you have us do? Sit around and bemoan our troubles to the Watching Dead?"

"Watch your mouth!"

Olivia covered her ears, moaning at the tremendous lack of perspective around her. It astounded her that anyone had the strength to argue after so much pain. They were either profoundly selfish or had incredible endurance. If the latter were true, then they should commit their energy to something more productive like the annual farm run, in happier days, where participants had to collect a sack of grain from as many different farms as they could in an eight-hour period without resorting to any powered forms of transport.

She wondered what her mother would say about the way those who had tried to use science to cheat fate were reacting now. Would she still think education was the solution to the troubles that plagued them? Her father believed more in the power of science, and would have had a difficult time relating to any of the claims made by the neo-religious fanatics.

Dad, why can't you be here, she thought, *to figure a way out. You tried to give us a gift, but why should my blood be any more worthy of moving through life's cycles than Faren's?* Her monologue was punctuated by the rising volume of outbursts as more and more people began shouting at each other. Turmoil seemed to seize everyone in the hold, releasing a contagious spread of discord.

Amid all the noise, a single voice started to cry out with more and more urgency, an alarm buried beneath layers of clamor. Olivia frowned as she sat up and looked around, searching for the source of the tremulous warning that threatened to be stifled like a candle in the wind. The cacophony rose as more people shouted and stood, the diversity of personal belief no longer providing a mosaic, but an arsenal for the self-destruction of the ship.

The absurdity of the situation made something bubble up inside Olivia.. She shook and clenched her fists to try and control herself, but the resulting tension spread to every corner of her body. She couldn't be the only one to see it, could she?

Standing up and feeling her limbs move of their own accord, Olivia wondered if this new energy stemmed from the same place as the human capacity for absurd bickering.

She took a deep breath, and began to shriek as loud as she could, as though the angry tremors in her body were the source of the sound. Everyone ducked and covered their ears. Olivia continued with her eyes closed until the piercing monotone was all that vibrated through her skull. The echo when she stopped wrapped around a silent and unmoving crowd who stared at her.

"Look at yourselves!" she shouted, before anyone could cut in. She wanted to shake the ship with her footsteps as she strode over to someone's pile of belongings, and snatched up a mirror. "Is this what you want to be?" She held the mirror high up in front of her, turning it toward one face after another as she stalked into the fray. "We've finally managed to get away from the evil that hunted us on Monitum, and you recreate it, reflecting it as surely as this mirror does your face."

"We haven't gotten away," said a woman's voice, small and distant at the back of the mob.

"What do you know? You're just a girl!"

"You think letting a child lead us will provide salvation? Only God—"

"ENOUGH!" screamed Olivia. "I will claw the eyes out of whoever speaks next, and if you doubt the sincerity of my rage due to my stature, I challenge you to test me." She glared at all around her, part of her wishing for the chance to release a boiling flood on the first person foolish enough to prod her. She could see right through false complaints as though they were irritating white noise, and she marveled that after all the refugees had been through, they still hadn't developed this awareness of atmosphere.

"Now, you," Olivia said, pointing past the crowd to a ghostly pale woman at the back. The woman who had been trying to give them a warning, to whom nobody had given the faintest attention. "Speak, unhindered."

The woman took a few moments to reply as people cleared away to make a path for her. She seemed to hold herself back from them as though they might jump her at any moment. "There are children attacking us," the woman stammered. "They were near the crew quarters, and are making their way through the ship." She swallowed, then blurted out, "Killing!"

Whispers fluttered through the crowd, and Olivia shushed them. A flicker of worry passed through her as she felt the implications of the attacking child warriors. "Where and how many?"

"I couldn't see," the woman said, falling to the side as blood seeped through her dress at the shoulder. "Enough, and with guns."

"She's hurt!"

Olivia saw that the woman had been shot. her backside was drenched in blood and her cheek bones etched hard lines into her pale complexion. "You," she snapped at a woman who had helped her care for Faren, "see to her. You three," she pointed to three boys, "help the injured move to a place they can be looked after."

"But the child warriors are unnatural highborns! Demon fighters! We can't win!"

"We have a few of our own. And we can outsmart them," Olivia said with such loud confidence it seemed to sever doubt with an icy edge. "The rest of you grab any weapons you have. Most experienced fighters up front. We push through and away from them, drawing them from their point of entry and where we can ambush them. Now, move!"

The change from the chaos, that had reined before, to the organized flurry that followed was like a grab rat transforming into a Monatese riding steed. The clatter of swords sang as they prepared for battle.

Olivia made sure there were capable guards at the rear, then she joined her band of defenders as they pressed forward through the labyrinth of the ship. A hushed silence fell over everyone as they watched for any sign of the child warriors.

They reached narrow hallways filled with control rooms for the ship's various functions. No one wanted to split up or be cornered where they could be slaughtered like cattle, so they all stayed together as they advanced on the bridge of the ship, past the crew quarters. The bridge proved to be a wide, gray patchwork of nervecloth displays and blinking indicators on three levels. The pilot, in a caged cockpit on the third level, sat with his back to them. In front of him, a semi-circle scoop of nervecloth showed the stars surrounding the jump to Gelion.

"Where are we?" Olivia asked, feeling her eyes bulge as she pushed through the crowd. "Excuse me, pilot, but what is that?" She pointed at the large display, noticing it was also flecked with the blue and red telemetry depicting ships. *It's a miracle we haven't collided with that swarm of ships,* she thought, swallowing hard.

The pilots said nothing, but continued managing the ship. He seemed tense.

Olivia frowned as she prepared another question. But before she could open her mouth again, someone signaled for attention. One of the younger boys whom she had caught trying to steal from the cargo bay shoved through to her position, panting, with a desperate look on his face.

"They're coming," he said, panting and darting a finger behind him. After a few breaths, he added, "Now."

Olivia couldn't will her body to kick in with adrenaline, as though she'd overstressed every muscle fiber for the next decade. Her skin tingled and something inside her hardened as she directed the strongest swordsmen to the entrances on two of the levels. The rest crouched behind the walls provided by the indicators and displays.

The ship rocked and jostled. Everyone struggled to maintain footing. Olivia realized their sanctuary — in the center of the storm displayed on the nervecloth — was no longer safe. Creaks and shudders resonated through the hollow cavity that housed the last survivors of the legacy that Laedan Ald'erda had started. Olivia readjusted her grip as her hands slickened with sweat. Suspicions about

Pleo were a sliver of fear that dug its way deep, threatening to break her focus on the rounded corner near the door. Anything else that came her way, however, she would meet headlong even if it meant death. *Faren, mother, father, I might be joining you soon.*

Two shadows crept around the corner. Young boys. They held pistols in one hand, swords in the other. They aimed for the pilot, and Olivia's breath caught. *What madness has taken you?*

The boys fired, and whooped, but their cries were stifled as the refugee warriors pounced. They had hesitated because the enemies were children, but as the ship rocked and swayed, their sympathy vanished.

The boys were crudely stripped of their weapons, the hands holding the guns slashed to force them to drop the *okal'a'ni* weapons. They whimpered in the corner as Olivia threatened them to keep quiet. She turned back to the door and saw a few more children — a boy, a girl and one more she could only see the shadow of — rounding the corner. This time, the children focused all their attention on firing their weapons, sending everyone scattering as a few refugees cried out in pain, their legs or arms struck by the tearing bullets.

"Stop! We are no threat to you!" Olivia shouted, barely able to hear herself. The children made no attempt to respond or to enter the room, and so she went and grabbed a dropped pistol and rolled it into the hallway from which the boys fired.

She had hoped the offering of the gun would make them pause, but all it did was inspire another round of bullets. The children had them pinned down in the bridge.

Olivia shook her head as her jaw tightened and tremors spread through her skull. *I. Am. So. Tired. Of. This.* Olivia grabbed the other young prisoner's pistol. She took it to one of the broken terminals and began firing at the base where it connected to the terminal. After a few seconds, the enemy stopped to pause at the strangeness of hearing gunshots but not seeing any of it directed their way.

Olivia didn't stop, however, until the terminal was ready to fall over. With a final kick and heave, she tore the terminal out its casing, plopping it down as she looked expectantly at a couple of refugees. "Shield!" she explained to them impatiently. With their help, she got it hauled up and in position.

On Olivia's count, they darted into the gunfire, the smash of metal-on-metal ringing in their ears as they surged forward, crying out as though trying to match the volume of the gunfire.

One of the children fell over on impact with the shield. The barrier pushed him aside like water diverted around a dam. He ended up sprawled on Olivia's side of the barrier. Immediately, one of the refugees dropped and slashed down at the young boy. He was no older than ten.

Olivia stopped pushing on the shield as her heart sank. She stared down at the blood. The two remaining children took advantage of the opportunity to surge back and tip the barrier over. It fell on top of Olivia, and she heard one of her helpers cry out as a child pumped bullets into him.

She heard another cry behind her.

"Stop, Olivia." The voice drove the sliver of fear deep into her as she gasped for breath. Her sword clattered to the floor. She wanted to tell herself the voice belonged to someone else, anyone else, but the harder she tried to deny the ugly truth, the more firm the conclusion became: it was Pleo.

She took short, shallow breaths through trembling lips. Her vision blurred and her body froze: the disquieting calm before a clear dream set in. The only thing that kept her anchored was her concern for her brother. "Pleo, what are you doing?" she whispered.

"I should be asking you the same question, sister," Pleo returned, his voice harsh and authoritative. "These adults you're harboring gave us this curse. And yet after all this you stand here defending them, almost to your dying breath."

Olivia turned her head slowly. She could see Pleo pointing a pistol at her. Behind him a handful of child warriors held pistols guarding the entrance to the bridge that now seemed light-years away.

"Pleo, they just wanted a better life," she said, her throat catching as her gaze faltered and she stared at the ground.

"They didn't mean to cause this, and we can end it here, right now. Kai'til's men are the enemy, not the people like Dad who—"

"Get up, and put your hands above your head," Pleo snapped. "I'm so disappointed, Olivia. You've been completely brainwashed by them. Even when Mom and Dad were alive, you believed Dad's song and dance. Where's Mom now? She believed he did nothing wrong, and paid the highest price."

Olivia was facing Pleo now, seeing the lines of stress, fatigue, and something monstrously joyful stratifying his face. She backed toward the bridge as Pleo and his gang followed slowly, in-step with an ominous cadence.

"Pleo, please," she said. "You're my brother. Let's stop right now and be a family again."

"You think I don't want that!?" Pleo screamed, leaning into her face as he kept the gun trained on her chest. "That's all I've ever wanted since Dad betrayed us all. You always thought you knew best, Olivia. You're wrong — so wrong — for siding with these people. They owe you their lives twice over. Once for handing you a lifetime of turmoil, and another for saving their skins. And what have they done for you? I come here to save you, to bring us all back together, and you act like I'm the one who's not seeing the whole picture?"

Olivia pressed her hands together, tears streaming down her cheeks. She shivered as flashes of a clear dream appeared on the edges of her vision. "Pleo, there will never be enough retribution to bring back or bring justice to Mom and Dad." She opened her hands in a welcoming gesture. "Which is why it has to stop."

Pleo sneered, the anguish finally showing through his dictator's facade. He and Olivia were now partway into the entrance, and he waved his pistol around at the cowering refugees. "Give up the adults, Olivia, and all the children will be spared."

Olivia blinked several times to refocus as her knees quivered. "No, Pleo. Everyone on this ship is going to stay alive. Including you, my dear brother." Whether out of the delirium that was creeping in because of the clear dream, or out of sheer desperation, she wasn't sure, but she tried a different tactic. "You remember when Dad took us on picnics in 'borrowed' vessels? Before Voltan was born? Why don't we just borrow this one?" She did her best to give a playful, mischievous look around. "I bet we can have a feast on Demora with how far this beauty'll take us." The words sounded like her father's, and she knew that she tread a thin line between Pleo's hatred and his need.

Pleo's gaze dropped down, looking through her at some distant memory. "Those were fun times," he said softly, his voice soothing.

The ship shuddered and Olivia didn't know if it was because the pilot was dead, or if the attacking *rel*-fighters had scored a major hit. It didn't matter— nothing was as important as regaining her brother.

"We always meant to bring Voltan with us," Pleo continued in reverie, "but Dad got so busy when he became Sheriff."

"Yeah, but there's still—"

Several things happened at once. Through the entrance of the second level of the bridge came Voltan and an emaciated, yet muscular man with a flat silver cap on his head. Pleo heard the commotion that the refugees made, and turned with his gun pointed upward toward the door. Olivia shrieked and pushed his weapon-arm with both hands before the trigger went off. The bullet's invisible trajectory ricocheted off the bridge's hullsteel ceiling, off two side walls and came sailing straight back toward Pleo.

A split second after Voltan and the man had entered the room, Olivia lay on top of an unmoving Pleo, a pool of blood draining from the back of his head where the bullet had struck. Olivia went into a spasm and she lost sight of everything in the room as agony took on new meaning.

Chapter 20

Voltan, with several takoshis in tow, entered the room with Prokhor, just as the lull inspired by Olivia and Pleo's reunion broke down in tragedy.

Refugee warriors rushed at them as the fighting broke out. When they were a meter away, Prokhor's hand flicked the eliox and his voice roared. "STOP!"

A hypnotic ring echoed off the hullsteel walls. Voltan felt his hands tingle. He did exactly as Prokhor instructed, pausing in mid-stride with his arms floating in the air. Strangely, though, the desire seemed to stem from within and a sense of relief overwhelmed the faint terror that scratched at the edge of his consciousness. The refugees had stopped in their tracks as well, swords raised as though time had frozen.

"Put down your weapons," Prokhor said, strolling by them as he continued to play the same eerie note on the eliox. The warriors put them down and stood neutral, looking at each other. Around the room swords clattered against the ship's floor. "You will not harm me," Prokhor went on, walking toward the center of the bridge. "Who here knows how to pilot?"

Several hands went up. Prokhor directed one to relieve the wounded pilot. And they complied smoothly, showing no resistance nor outward signs of being manipulated. The rocking ship steadied.

One of the cowering adults, the only people unaffected by the eliox, suddenly charged at Prokhor.

"You," Prokhor pointed at one of the children who had nearly skewered him a moment ago, "kill him."

As Prokhor darted out of the way, the Monatese child attacked the desperate adult. The child's ferocity was unrelenting. A few seconds later the adult lay on the ship's floor.

"I trust the rest of you will not be as foolish," Prokhor said, smiling with a sneer as he strode past the fearful adults. He went on to learn every single child's name, and commanded them as though they were chess pieces. Pleo's surviving child warriors only added to the ranks, and were just as complacent.

"Land on Gelion," Prokhor instructed, a twisted grin on his face as he cradled the eliox, and capitalized on the inhaled protein to control all of his "toys".

Voltan stood with the takoshis lined up complacently behind him, and watched everything unfold as though he himself had wanted the same outcome. Buried deep within, however, part of him was screaming with horror at what he had unleashed upon everyone he loved.

In the space between spaces, a soul drifted as particles washed around it, scraping away and eroding it bit by bit. The fragment of humanity was far from a full being, and its presence so minute most *rel*-skimmers would never notice it was there. For the soul fragment to be touched in any way, someone had to know what he was looking for.

A gentle hand washed over everything, and nearly brushed past the chunk as others had before. The fragment could not respond, could not reach out or react in any way, so the hand went past and the soul kept drifting. The hand passed it again, but this time paused and enveloped it, cradling and sheltering it from the indifference of the cosmos.

The hand pulse with intention and deeper meaning, but it flowed like electricity through an overpowered transistor, creating heat and destroying the precious balances that maintained its state of existence. Recognizing this, the being eased off, focusing purely on transporting the fragment. It took a steady mind controlling the hand to commit so fully to the feeling without letting selfish desires bubble beneath the surface.

The being brought the fragment toward a dense cluster, weaving through the debris until it approached a shape that evoked a primitive form of familiarity. As the hand pushed through to the core, the fragment came alive, pulsing with an inner light that amplified through pure proximity to a source, a network. The cascading growth spread to fill the form which both was and was not separate from everything around it.

Nestor Tark gasped as he awakened in his *rel*-fighter, his body aching with the pain of oxygen starvation. His teeth chattered and he shivered as oxygen returned to his blue veins, and his muscles started reversing the process that had already begun hardening them. He screamed in pain as he shifted in his straps, movement sending sharp acidic flashes through his nervous system.

His ears rang for some time, until he began to notice words repeated over and over again, with unrelenting monotony.

"Nestor, please respond," came Di Mon's flat voice. "Nestor, respond."

Tentatively stretching out his hand, wincing as he rotated his arm, Nestor touched the transmitter. "Nuh," he croaked, the passage of air making him gasp for another breath. He took a few breaths with his eyes closed and sucked on the tube of the water bottle beside his head before trying again. "Nestor here."

"Welcome back, my friend," Di Mon said, his relief palpable despite his attempt to sound casual. "Can you fly?"

Nestor wasn't sure if he'd be able to do anything again, but he slowly wrapped his hands around the controls. "I can try."

"We need to board the freighter," Di Mon explained. "If you can see my wake, follow me."

Nestor did as instructed, the facts coming back to him slowly through the movement and re-established homeostasis of his bloodstream. Moving robotically, he followed the rel-fighter he supposed was Di Mon, and eventually found himself bringing his ship to dock. Nestor frowned as he struggled to remember where he was. They were in a well-traveled space lane, and shouldn't be docking with a freighter under sub-light power. It all felt wrong and dangerous, and his hands jerked at the controls. He relaxed a bit when he saw a few ward ships trundling along at 1-g acceleration, as good as stationary from the perspective of reality skimming.

Nestor dropped his ship with a bump to the dock floor, and lowered his head onto his arms, wondering if he would ever move again. Di Mon's banging on the hatch of his ship was the only reason he dragged himself out of his flight harness. When he opened the door, Di Mon looked him up and down, noticing the patches of bruises and burst blood vessels all over any exposed skin surfaces.

"You look like you need more sleep, yourself," Nestor said, to preempt criticism. "You were never cut out for being liege."

Di Mon glared at him, then stepped forward and hugged him. "You tell anyone I hugged you and I'll kill you," he whispered, cheerfully, before he stepped back. "Thank the gods you're alive."

"No, thank you," Nestor said, patting his friend on the back. His mind still felt a bit murky but he knew that the passage he had just taken would not have been possible without a friend as strong-minded and disciplined as Di Mon. "I owe you everything."

"You owe me a sword-hand," Di Mon said, letting go of him and reaching for Nestor's sword-strap inside the ship. "This is uglier than anything we ever could have imagined. And I'm not even sure I understand the whole thing."

Nestor had flashes of what had occurred prior to being dunked, and trembled. "All I can imagine is ugly right now," he said quietly. "Did the others make it?"

Di Mon shook his head. "A few fled back to Monitum. The rest..." He gazed into the distance, picturing the lost souls shattered by the child warriors. "Let's go," he said as his voice caught, trying to mask the pain on his face by turning toward the door. Together they raced off through the empty hallways of the ship.

Nestor's sense of time was like the market queues in UnderGelion, a hodgepodge of faces and orders that were carried out in a manner whose logic only the gods understood. Di Mon's vest whipped around as he skirted corners and Nestor followed, wondering if his hand would remember how to hold a sword.

"Di Mon," said Nestor, "where's Enid?"

The question stopped his friend in his tracks, and he turned to face the confused and stricken Nersallian.

"I saw him race off to make a jump, in the direction of Monitum," Di Mon said, scanning Nestor's face. "It was right after he dunked you. The other child pilots followed him."

Nestor's brow creased as he searched for his memory for a clue as to what Enid's flight meant. "Were they done?"

"There were a few of Kai'til's followers left. I dispatched them."

"Then it was something else."

"Nestor," Di Mon said, stopping to put his hands on Nestor's shoulders. "Everyone in the shake-up could feel it when he dunked you."

"Is that... how you found me?" Nestor asked.

Di Mon nodded. "Although he's not the only one who knew you, I think it must have hit Enid harder than anyone." Di Mon released him. "I don't know what Enid's actions mean, but right now we need to stop this ship before it gets underway, again, for Gelion. If that is, indeed, where it is headed."

Nestor nodded, accepting his duty with a strange sense of sagacity. He and Di Mon pressed on until they could hear the scuttle of feet along the floor, and — to Nestor's horror — the Caddy's voice giving orders.

Before Di Mon could whisper instructions, Nestor had walked right into the bridge. The eerie calm on all the children as they guarded the crouching and fearful adults, as well as the Caddy perched atop the lookout platform with takoshis scattered all about, gave the scene a surreal quality.

Two children moved toward Nestor as he strode directly toward the Caddy.

"Stop him," said the Caddy without turning around, as the eliox rang through the room.

The children jumped in front of Nestor and crossed their swords in his path, the weapons almost as tall as they were. Nestor stopped, and looked at the children's faces. They didn't appear to be struggling or manipulated.

"Why are you listening to him?" he asked.

"He just suggests what makes sense," said one. The children didn't move.

The skin on the back of Nestor's neck bristled. "Caddy, how about we leave the children out of this, and you and I have a chat among friends?"

The Caddy laughed. "Nestor, your offer is appreciated." He turned to face him, the smile vanishing into a menacing sneer. "But we both know you're in no position to bargain. You're in more of a position to beg."

With expert fluidity and ease, the Caddy ushered commands and had Nestor surrounded.

"Get the man in the corridor," he added, and soon Di Mon was brought in alongside Nestor.

"You were supposed to be my backup," said Nestor.

"I thought you were mine," growled Di Mon.

"Welcome, Liege Monitum!" the Caddy exclaimed. "It seems the only one we're missing is the awful Kai'til."

"You picked him," said Nestor, goose bumps covering his skin at the realization of how much puppetry had been going on from the start. "You orchestrated all of this."

"Yes, but that wasn't because I liked him. You have to use the right tool for the job, you see, but the tool is not always a pretty one."

Di Mon shot Nestor a glance indicating that he wanted to fight back, but Nestor didn't respond. He wouldn't harm the children no matter what, and he wondered if that, too, had factored into the Caddy's grand plan.

"Why Gelion, Prokhor?" Di Mon demanded.

The Caddy's face darkened upon the mention of his real name. "You've done some homework. How, I don't know, but you won't live long enough for it to be of any significance. Because we're among friends," he said with a wink and a step in their direction, "I'll let you know how much the empire has to look forward to when you've joined the Watching Dead. I've heard they don't see as much as their name implies."

With a sweeping gesture to the loyal children around him, the Caddy continued. "These children are Monatese high-borns, as I'm sure you know, and remarkably, they have some of the same brain chemistry as my dear takoshis." He walked over and picked one of the animals up from the ground. "The very intelligent Voltan, here, helped me figure out the last piece of the puzzle about how to control them all." He patted Voltan, who smiled absently.

"The empire will never know what hit it when these children arrive. Oh, we'll go slowly at first. I can't risk them being executed on the spot as freaks who can't be trusted. We might establish ourselves as Vrellish highborns, for a few years, or lie low until the children are a little older."

Nestor wondered how he could get at the Caddy without seriously injuring any of the children. "I thought Dartha ordered you to take them to Sanctuary," he said.

The Caddy raised an eyebrow. "My, my, you're almost an even match for your friend from Green Hearth in intel, now, Nestor. I'm so proud." He licked his lips, and the next words out of his mouth were harsh. "The Lorels think they're better than everyone. Dartha thinks the only useful function I have is in subservience. They are about to learn how wrong they are. Not only will I beat them at their own game, but I'll go further than their feeble chess-play from the sidelines.

"It's too bad, Nestor, that you won't live long enough to call me Ava." The Ava was head of the empire, commanding ultimate power over all Sevildom. Nestor shivered.

Creasing his brow, the Caddy rubbed his chin. "Liege Monitum, I might keep you around to help out. I wouldn't have to pretend the children were exotic Red Reach Vrellish if you helped me come up with a good story. You are nearly as good at manipulating your fellow lieges, after all, as I am."

"I'm flattered," replied Di Mon in a cold tone.

"You should be."

"What if the Gelacks discover what you are and what you've done?" Nestor needed more time. He hoped that the children would shift enough for him to have an opening. He stepped to the side but was prodded back into the center of the circle.

"There will doubtless be a duel," the Caddy said, a smile growing on his face. "And I'll fix it so my side wins." He rubbed his fingers together as if some trick, or magic powder, lay between them. "Or apply some judicious assassinations mixed, maybe, with some character smears to discredit the honorable. Marry a child or two into some good Demish houses…" He trailed off as he mused, enjoying the possibilities.

Di Mon darted forward but the children slashed his arms and chest, drawing fine lines of red across his vestments.

The ship shuddered into *rel*-skimming mode once more.

"Ah, we're underway again," the Caddy said with a sigh. "I debated whether it was worth the delay of playing dead to entice you both to land. So pleased it proved worthwhile. But the future calls! It's so exciting." He turned to face

Nestor and Di Mon again, his neck craning forward until he looked like he was hunching. In this position the unnatural way his arm connected to his body was prominent, the clusters of muscles pulling at his chest and shoulder in a way that made him seem inhuman. "But now we must say a final goodbye."

Chapter 21

Remei lay tied to a large four-poster, canopied bed with a hard-wood canopy top, the wire binding cutting into her wrists and ankles. She had memorized the stains and swirls in the wood of the canopy covering. Except for a servant coming in to feed her, Kai'til had left her alone and tied up here for some time now. She was grateful that his threats of death to anyone who touched her before he did had held enough sway that she'd escape random molestation.

She'd stopped struggling when she realized how hopeless it was, and reserved her energy for the inevitable moment when Kai'til would try to use her. It was all she could think of at this point, since she couldn't bear to dwell on how she had failed the children. Perhaps if she dealt with Kai'til, they would all come back. She wanted to believe they would.

Kai'til opened the door and the air seemed to suck out of the room. "Hello, pretty," he said, running his tongue along bared teeth. "I'm sorry I've neglected you for so long. So much on the go. I'm sure you understand."

Remei said nothing.

"Now, now, are you giving me the cold shoulder? Are you like a sad puppy whose owner has left him alone for too long? Well, don't worry, we'll fix that soon enough." He stripped out of his clothes, and approached her in his undergarments.

"Still smell fresh," he cooed as he straddled her helpless body. "I'm glad the girl I assigned to the job's been taking care of you." He began to yank at her meager clothing, not caring if he roughed her up in the process. Remei remained silent as he climbed on top of her. Clenching her fists, she tried to steel herself for the coming pain as she pressed her hips lower into the mattress.

"I hardly need preparation, you're so lovely," Kai'til said. "Why I—"

Remei thrust upward as hard as she could, capitalizing on the mattress springs to send Kai'til high enough that he smacked the top of the bed canopy. Grunting, he fell forward, his head falling into hers. Ignoring the thudding pain as he made contact, she turned her head and sank her teeth hard into his nose. His hands had dropped close enough to hers that she could dig her nails into his wrists, and she could feel the blood ooze out as Kai'til howled in pain. She would have kneed him if she wasn't splayed out.

"Help!" he screamed, his feet kicking futilely as he was forced to lie flat against her. "Kill her! NOW!"

Remei could hear the stomping of boots as they came down the hallway toward her. She clenched her jaw harder into Kai'til's nose, the metallic taste of blood slipping over her tongue. It was doubtful she would make it out of this alive, but if some small bit of justice could be brought forth out of the destruction, that would be enough to justify the effort.

The pounding footsteps ticked away the inevitability of the situation. She thought of how she had arrived almost at the cusp of the rebellion Di Mon had hoped to hide from the rest of the Empire. If anyone did find out, all of Monitum would be purged under the Empire's collective scorn. But was that any worse than what was happening now? She had tried to protect the children, tried to protect everyone, and had still been left gasping for air in a tumultuous sea she knew was far more complicated and twisted than she'd ever imagined.

As Kai'til's struggles became weaker, she wondered if any history books would describe what happened, as a forewarning to the coming generations. She wanted to make sure her children would never be a part of anything this soul-sickening, but even that request seemed a faint dream now.

The door burst open and someone shoved Kai'til off her. He landed with a moan beside the bed. Remei caught a glimpse of a raised sword, and screamed as she realized she couldn't move enough to dodge the blade that plunged toward her chest.

Someone shoved the guard forward and he missed, impaling the mattress beside her. A blade went through the guard, eliciting a strangled gasp. Growling, Kai'til reached up onto the bed and snatched the blade from the fallen guard. He attacked the unexpected assailant with ferocity. As the metal flashed and the guard fell out of the way, Remei could hardly believe her eyes: it was Enid.

Kai'til slashed Enid in the shoulder as he spun away just in time, colliding with a wall in the cramped space. The series of parries and ripostes became a blur to Remei as she tried to follow what was happening. She dared not cry out for fear of distracting her son, but her sense of helplessness slowly eroded what remained of her sanity. She wondered if she had indeed gone over the edge, and her mind had just come up with an elaborate way of distracting her throughout the full duration of Kai'til's torture.

Cackling in triumph as his blade slashed Enid's cheek and nose, Kai'til slowed for a second. It was enough time for Enid to slash at the lamp above Kai'til's head, which came crashing down on top of him. A moment later, Enid had disarmed him and held his sword to Kai'til's throat.

"Mom, close your eyes," Enid said, his voice steeled to hide the pain of his oozing wounds.

"Don't, Enid," Remei said, unwilling to see her son carry out the ugly but necessary act.

"He was about to—"

"He will pay for what he's done. But you don't have to dirty your soul with his blood. A public hearing and execution will be fitting for everyone to see that this sick rat is dead for good."

"My legacy will live on," Kai'til croaked.

"The only thing that will be remembered, if anything," Remei spat as her son grabbed Kai'til by the throat, "is how we defeated you."

With that, Enid gave him a walloping smack with the hilt of his sword, and he slumped into unconsciousness, bleeding from a scalp wound.

As Enid cut his mother's bonds and helped her into her clothes, she could not stop staring at him. She tore off part of her sleeve and dabbed at his face, tending to his wounds and running her hands through his hair until he pushed her away in embarrassment.

"Is it really you?" she asked breathlessly.

"Yes, Mom, who else could it be?"

"How in the gods did you find me?"

Enid's face grew serious, then twisted in pain before he helped her up. "I'll tell you when we get out of here."

They made it out of Kai'til's lair safely, Enid having dispatched most of the ill-trained militia guards on the way in. The few that remained were not loyal enough to continue fighting in the face of a fatal determination. Not when things had started going badly for Kai'til since Di Mon's fleet troops arrived.

As they walked the empty, damaged streets of Grianach, Enid began to tell Remei what had happened, up to the hazy sensations that had brought him back from total darkness. Remei knew at once what Nestor had done for their son, because no one in the universe could have soul-touched Enid so deeply. She whispered the suggestion with tears in her eyes, and Enid's face lit up in recognition, then horror. In an abandoned bar, they sat and wept together, the release of tension ushering in a torrent of emotion.

Voltan moved in, slowly, on Nestor and Di Mon, approaching the inner circle of children who slashed almost playfully at the two highborn Sevolites. Teasing and tormenting them. Di Mon seized a sword near the hilt and yanked it from his child-tormentor's grasp. He might have killed the boy with a retaliating blow if Nestor hadn't cried out and interfered with him. At the same time, Nestor used his back to block Di Mon from another cut.

Di Mon cursed.

"They're children!" said Nestor, wincing at the sting of his cuts.

After a quick attack on his wrist, Di Mon lost the captured sword. He stumbled back into Nestor, holding the bleeding hand and grimacing. There were simply too many armed children.

Prokhor laughed at the men's helplessness as he surrounded them in the maelstrom of human consciousness controlled by his eliox.

"Voltan, cut Nestor in the shin," he said, a gleeful tone in his voice.

As before, the thought seemed as though it was Voltan's own. He pushed through the children that encircled the two men,, and drew a gash in Nestor's leg. He could see the resignation in his surrogate father's face, a strange, stoic integrity that Nestor would probably maintain until the last drop of his blood had spilled.

Prokhor's laughter echoed through the bridge as the ship entered the Reach of Gelion and headed toward the planet. "You know what the best part of this all is?"

Nestor and Di Mon both said nothing.

"That you probably would be able to get out of this if you really wanted to, but you won't." Prokhor stalked into the crowd of children, getting very close to the inner circle as he leered at the two highborns. "Come on, they're just children. You could strike them down without any effort."

Di Mon looked at Nestor, then surged forward again. Barking commands, Prokhor had Di Mon seized and pinned to the ground within seconds. He howled with elation as Di Mon cried out.

Voltan watched with a frown on his face, the lingering feeling in the back of his mind growing a little without a command to confuse everything. He thought back to the work he had done making the neurotransmitter, and tried to visualize the network of reactions in order to find a way out.

The interface depended upon the note that was being played on the eliox, which established a neurological basis for the reaction in the inner lobes. It was the electrical stimulus that could be kept more or less constant, and serve as a platform from which a variety of commands and suggestions could be given.

That was it. Cupping his hands over his ears and humming loudly to himself, Voltan could barely hear the ring of the eliox now. He crouched down to avoid being seen. As

Prokhor laughed maniacally after issuing a further attack, Voltan made his move.

Arrogantly, Prokhor still rang the eliox as the two Sevolites writhed on the ground in front of him. He didn't notice Voltan's disobedience. Voltan took a deep breath, humming a Monatese folksong to himself, then yelled, "Everyone sleep now!"

It was a longshot that the hormonal and neurochemical balances for sleep could be induced so quickly, but it worked. The children all slumped and fell to the ship floor, their weapons clattering as Prokhor screamed at them to awaken. He played the eliox as loud as he could, and as a few of the children stirred, Voltan unclamped his hands and dove.

Prokhor shouted at him to stop, and his vision wavered as doubt crept into his mind. He hummed the folksong even louder, stimulating his auditory cortex on his own as he crashed into Prokhor and knocked his hand off the eliox.

They struggled for several moments, the crash and bang of notes a shrieking cacophony that served to better awaken the children. Voltan wrenched the eliox away from Prokhor as a foot planted itself on the Caddy's chest.

"This ends now, Prokhor," said a woman's voice. Voltan looked up to see a woman of average build and average height, with brown hair and brown eyes, standing over him. She was wearing white flight leathers marked in jeweled DNA strands. Voltan didn't know where she'd come from, but he guessed she must be Prokhor's Lorel master. Unless he had lied about that, too. A taste of bitter regret entered his mouth as he rolled away and stared at master and pupil.

"You thought you could get away with this all by yourself?" she demanded.

Prokhor struggled, but she pushed him back down. "I gave you an opportunity," she said with a sigh, "and you breached every bit of trust I ever placed in you."

"Every bit of pretentious arrogance you heaped upon me?" he spat. "There were always limits to the leash you kept around me, Dartha."

She smiled. "Everyone's on a leash, Prokhor. Even me."

The thought made Voltan shudder. He noticed several takoshis crawling their way to the center of the bridge.

Prokhor was practically frothing at the mouth, his head bobbing as he snarled. "The order you so preciously hold dear will come to an end. Sooner or later, all the Sevolites in the empire will make the same discoveries I did about how to make highborns. And the desire for power will far outweigh the fear of upsetting *Okal Rel*, as we saw so easily on Monitum. Your tenuous control of the status quo will rock and tip out of control.

"With or without me, the empire will eat itself. I just wanted to get the best seat to watch it happen." Prokhor, the Caddy, closed his mouth and glared at Dartha, who watched casually as the takoshis skittered toward their creator.

"Letting you make these creatures was my first mistake," Dartha said with a sigh, shaking her head. "You think we exercise little influence on Sevildom out of arrogance? It is out of profound respect for the powers of individual conscience." She pointed a finger at Voltan, who shrank away as he wrapped his arms around the eliox. "Your pupil outwitted you despite everything you laid in place. Kai'til's egotistical reign of terror spun too far out of control for the parameters we gave you."

Prokhor heaved and Dartha withdrew her foot from his chest, giving the illusion that he could stand and walk away. As though she had known with clarity what was to happen, the takoshis jumped on top of him, their claws and teeth tearing his flesh as he screamed.

Voltan's hand hovered over the eliox. He could stop all of Prokhor's pain with a flick of his wrist, but felt repulsed by the idea of controlling the takoshis again. Prokhor had made them and treated them like playthings, when their brain chemistry was advanced enough for the lizards to make their own decisions. In respect for the free will and choice that he had watched snatched away, Voltan closed his eyes and did nothing.

"Voltan!" Prokhor cried as he writhed on the ground. "Voltan, please! You were my favorite! I never intended to use you. Please, my little friend, please..."

A few minutes later, Prokhor's cries stopped as the takoshis continued working on his corpse. Dartha strolled over to Voltan. "Make them stop," she said.

"No."

"It's repulsive," she said, shooting a glance over her shoulder, "and he's dead."

"Many things are repulsive, but they don't give me permission to play as a god."

Dartha sighed. "Fine. Pilot, take us to dock at the nearest Monatese station. Now."

The pilot did as instructed, turning back within sight — on his nervecloth — of the ward ships from the jump coming out to parley with them. The pilot, who was a Monatese woman, was too shocked by all she'd lived through in the last hour to ask questions of anyone. All the Monatese were awestruck in the terrifying presence of a Lorel, but knew that the burden of explaining everything that had occurred to the Ava and the rest of Fountain Court would fall upon Di Mon. Some of the children were so thoroughly confused they sat down where they found themselves standing, and those of the younger ones — who weren't too Vrellish to be incapable of it — began to cry.

"Adults, take the children," Dartha ordered. "Leave the weapons here and go to the cargo hold."

There were some altercations with Pleo's surviving child warriors, but with Pleo dead they didn't last long. Friends and relatives shepherded lost children silently away from the bridge, and although the room cooled down noticeably after they left, the smell of blood remained. Voltan ran his fingers through his sister's hair, his other hand resting on Pleo's cold leg. "Wake up, Olivia," he whispered, tears in his eyes. His sister stirred, and gave a gasp as she realized Pleo lay beneath her.

"I did this," she said, recoiling away from her dead brother. She huddled on the cold floor with her arms around her knees, squeezing her eyes and shaking her head.

"No, you didn't," Voltan said, his words breaking up as he held back tears. "It was Pleo's way of being wrong. Like your clear dreams and my thinking. That's what killed him." He took a seat beside her and did his best to wrap his arms around her.

The two children pressed together, their chests pushing against one another as they each took heaving gasps to try and satiate their grief.

"Di Mon, come with me," Dartha said.

Di Mon paused in the act of stemming the blood from his many, shallow wounds. He merely nodded, and began limping toward the door. Nestor moved to come along, but Dartha put up her hand. "Him only."

"You'll have to kill me to stop me. It's happened once already today, and the Watching Dead have an annoying habit of kicking me back here."

"He comes," Di Mon said, his throat hoarse.

Dartha narrowed her eyes at one then the other, and shrugged. "Fine," she said to Nestor. "You'll wish you hadn't."

Voltan stirred, and before they could all leave him, shouted for help. "Please help carry my sister, Nestor."

Nestor responded instantly to the request, but handed Olivia to one of the stronger refugees herding the children out. Voltan thanked him, but when he didn't move to follow the other children, Nestor gave him a puzzled look.

"Er— thanks, Nestor," Voltan said, putting his head down and turning.

Nestor touched the child on his shoulder before wrapping his arms around him in a warm hug. "Things will get better," he whispered. "I promise."

Voltan nodded and moved off. Nestor watched him for a few seconds, then followed Di Mon and Dartha into one of the crew quarters. He didn't notice that Voltan had turned back and was also following them, not intending to be left in the dark any longer.

"So," Dartha said once they were inside the room, bunk beds on each far wall with a few pieces of furniture in the middle. "I think we can all agree that Sevildom must never learn of what happened here."

Nestor spat out a stream of curses. "Sevildom can learn about the pettiness of our genetic hierarchy, for starters," he said, feeling as though his recent return from death had given him fresh perspective.

"That's not what they'll learn," Di Mon replied, shaking his head sadly. "They'll just come to Monitum and kill us all."

"He's right," said Dartha. "If there are two reactions to a given situation which either maintain or disturb the status quo, maintenance will always be more readily chosen."

Nestor looked at both of them, knowing that they were right but wishing there were some way around it, some loophole or trick that could be used to make all the sacrifices have meaning. There were black armchairs bolted to the floor, but no one sat. "So how do you propose to make this go away?" Di Mon asked.

"We erase everyone's memory of what happened."

Nestor stared at her for several seconds. Even Di Mon jumped a little, although he didn't seem quite as surprised. "Are you joking?"

Dartha's face was unflinching. "Not in the least."

"That's absurd," Nestor went on, shaking his head. "You can't do that. The ramifications... the ripple of memory throughout the mind... there's just no way. You'll damage everyone so badly you might as well kill them."

"Would you rather we do that? I assure you, it'd be easier."

"You're ridiculous! If those are the only two options then I say we leave things as they are and accept the retribution that Sevildom may unleash."

Di Mon once more shook his head, and gave a tired sigh. "No, Nestor, it's not that simple. Some will try to kill us, but others will try to steal the highborn-creating technology for themselves."

"Not only that," added Dartha, "this conflict has resulted in many bifurcations of the *Okal Rel* doctrine. Where before belief was a public, tangible thing shared by all and relatively easily managed, now there are several private religions beginning to fester on this ship alone. Another sin of our ancestors was a diversity of conflicting religions that helped justify total war."

Nestor held his tongue,˙ thinking, *All you want is to keep Sevolites controllable by the Lorels.* But he was tired. And balanced against the ill-defined resentment was a huge potential for the loss of life.

The room went quiet, the whirring of air through ducts the only sign of any movement. Dartha broke the silence first. "We don't have much time to decide, because I need to make the preparations if this is to be done safely."

Nestor frowned. His chest felt heavy with the weight of worries that the Lorel seemed to promise might be washed away. "You can't do it without damaging them," he said, stubbornly.

"My pupil just took puppet control of an entire generation, and still you doubt me?" Dartha said, in her mild and unflappable manner.

Nestor stared at the Lorel and resisted the urge to tremble. There was so much the Lorels were responsible for, and now that he knew they were still around, lurking behind the scenes… it was almost too much. Part of him wanted to check out, go lose himself to gap and forget the universe until some semblance of sense returned. Maybe it never would, though.

The Lorels were known for being cunning and ruthless, and if the Caddy was any indication of what they were capable of, then the Empire had a lot to be afraid of. Nestor imagined that the only reason Sevildom had been allowed to continue as it had was because the Lorels allowed it, and wondered if the day would ever come when they lost interest, got bored, or worse— began to fear them.

"You've accepted this, Di Mon?" Nestor asked.

Di Mon strode two steps and took a seat in one of the comfortable chairs fixed to the floor, physical relief washing over him. "I have."

"So what are you going to tell Gelion when the troops come marching?"

Dartha cut in. "Liege Monitum will keep more of his memories of what happened in Grianach."

Nestor turned toward her. "Then let me keep mine."

"No." Dartha's voice was flat. "There's no need. Di Mon will have to resolve the problems in Grianach, and he'll need to know enough to do it sensibly." She looked at Di Mon. "Besides, he has a vested interest in making sure this stays a secret. Monitum is the only planet that still maintains trade with the Lorels, and that could be cut off quite sharply if word gets out. So it is only my presence, and what's transpired here with Prokhor that he'll forget. If he was too blank about events on Monitum it would be hard for him to contain them."

Nestor's jaw clenched. "So you admit that the rest of us will be a bunch of hollow shells."

Dartha shrugged. "You'll be everything you were before you came to Grianach," she said. And indulged in a mild look of amusement at Nestor's expense. "It will not be my doing if what you were amounted to a 'hollow shell'."

Di Mon rubbed his forehead and nodded. "If this is your price for sparing Monitum disgrace, so be it," he said.

"Then it's decided," said Dartha.

Nestor knew it was pointless to continue bickering, so he gave a slight nod, having no intention of following through on Dartha's plan.

He didn't remember what happened next.

Di Mon was there when Nestor awoke.

"Nestor," Di Mon said. He turned from the plastiglass window looking out onto space near the jump to the Reach of Gelion.

Di Mon's face was marked by two fresh cuts, just starting to heal. Acting on some instinct, Nestor raised his own arms and found similar marks on his forearms. Shifting in bed, he could feel his leg was bandaged. He could not remember how any of it had happened, but noticing Di Mon rub his wrist, he had a powerful, instinctive insight that whatever it was, it had happened to both of them.

"I know," Di Mon said, gravely, and came over to sit down by Nestor's bed. He touched his own face. "I don't… quite remember." He paused a moment. "You?"

Nestor tried to process a series of emotional impressions: fear, outrage, exhaustion and despair. "No," he admitted, unable to decode anything.

"Nestor—" Di Mon put a hand on his arm. The contact felt too meaningful. Both sensed it. Di Mon wet his thin lips in a self-conscious gesture and lifted his hand away. "Tell me what you remember," he asked. "In particular, since coming to the Grianach spaceport on Monitum."

When Nestor finished his short recollection, Di Mon added what he knew himself. His description painted a picture of mob violence in Grianach District on Monitum sparked by accusations Laedan Ald'erda, Di Mon's district sheriff and master of the spaceport, was implicated in a contraband drug scandal. "Whatever the drugs Laedan Ald'erda and his wife were peddling," he concluded, "they had a Lorel contact. A contact who has been in touch with me via our usual connections with TouchGate Hospital, who is apologetic about dangerous drugs getting into the Ald'erdas' hands, and is offering advice and free supplies for treatments of those suffering from psychotic side effects." He paused. "It is hard to know what to believe. I have a few, scattered memories. Images and impressions really. Things that don't make sense."

He looked at Nestor. "Do you remember the last week?"

"No." Nestor stroked the healing slashes on his own arm. "So you and I must have been affected."

"Yes," Di Mon said. His thin lips pressed together. "Except I am quite sure I would never have taken anything like the serum concerned. And I can't believe you would have, either."

"Doesn't add up," Nestor mumbled.

"Unless there was some element of contagion, as my TouchGate correspondent suggests," Di Mon said. "Apparently, for a period of limited duration, some of the psychotic side effects could manifest in anyone who inhaled the exhalations of a dosed person."

Nestor lay back and groped for his own images and impressions that didn't fit into memories of the days before his coming to Grianach. "Enid," he said, with a sudden start of sharp anxiety. "And Remei!"

"They are both fine," Di Mon assured him. "I've had word about them from Monitum." He frowned. "Although

I've deduced your son's supposed grab rat is a contraband fighting beast from an UnderDocks gambling ring."

Nestor waited, prepared to defend Enid's right to keep Cam if Di Mon tried to confiscate the takoshi.

But Di Mon didn't bother. Instead, he looked awkward. "What I think I remember," he said, "is... quite absurd."

"What?" Nestor asked, eager to fill in the sense of absence in his head.

Di Mon frowned. "So absurd," he stressed, "that if you don't remember it, I am prepared to believe we've each suffered separate hallucinations, with some real life consequences we are lucky to have survived. You've been flying hard. A freighter full of deranged people near exhaustion was en route to Gelion, littered with nearly as many handguns as swords — obtained from I know not where — and half the people on board are dead, killed by each other. And then there's these," he said, touching his face. "Both of us have been cut in a dozen places each. As if we were running a gauntlet."

"What do you remember?" Nestor asked, his voice growing more serious.

"I—" Di Mon began, and couldn't seem to get the words out. "It is truly absurd," he said, again, disturbed by whatever clue he felt he needed to reveal.

"Tell me," Nestor insisted.

Di Mon balked again. But the seriousness of the situation overcame his reluctance. "I... remember seeing you naked. You and Remei," he added, quickly. "You were brought to me by an errant captain. Naked."

Nestor stared back at him, thinking there was no safe way to tell his friend he had to forgive his subconscious for the nature of his personal hallucinations. Although he was a little disturbed to know Remei had also featured in Di Mon's drugged dreams.

"Do you remember anything like that?" Di Mon asked, sharply.

"Uh, no," said Nestor.

There was a long pause. And then they both said, slightly out of phase with each other, "Psychotic side effects."

Chapter 22

Voltan stared out at the rising Monatese sun that cast long shadows on the people in queues to be treated. The story, which everyone had been fed, was that there were some long-term side-effects of the highborn serum "cure-all" that affected anyone who either had obtained it through Ald'erda connections, or had come into contact with anyone who had. In other words, everyone. The threat of infection was real enough for people to line up in droves for the treatment that would prevent them suffering the psychiatric side-effects of paranoia.

Side effects, Voltan thought grimly, *was a mild way to put it.* An understatement of the violence that had resulted in so many needless deaths and had paralyzed life in Grianach for the duration of its grip on the populace. Some refused to believe they'd experienced delusions during the outbreak, but as more and more of their neighbors got the treatment, they began to sound like the crazy ones.

Turning the vial in his hands, Voltan looked at Olivia finally asleep in her bed. She looked much more beautiful now than she did awake, because she wasn't crying or wracked with the pain of far more troubles than should be accorded to a girl so young.

Voltan had gone back to Prokhor's lair almost immediately after returning, and tried to fashion a substance that would counter any memory-altering effects. He had found enough reference material to come up with something that essentially took a chemical snapshot of the brain, then chemically maintained it over the process of several hours. It wasn't guaranteed to work, since he didn't have access to the Lorel technology in Prokhor's lair for very long. The next time he went back, everything was gone. But it was worth a shot.

The trouble was, several crucial inorganic ingredients were in short supply, and nearly impossible to synthesize.

Voltan had scoured the lab in his efforts to find them, but had come up with nothing. The most he could make with what Prokhor had left him was a single vial. One person would remember all that had happened when the treatments were over.

Olivia stirred and slowly opened her eyes. "Voltan?" she murmured.

"Morning," he said, a faint smile on his lips.

They stared at one another for a moment, savoring the rare occasions when they just enjoyed life. As the silence lengthened, Voltan exhaled. "How are you feeling?"

Olivia just nodded, and said nothing.

"Listen," he began, walking across the room and sitting on her bed, "there's something important I have to tell you. Are you awake? I can wait until after breakfast if you want."

Olivia sat up straight, propping herself against her pillow as she rubbed her eyes. "No, I'm awake. Go ahead. Full attention."

Voltan took a deep breath. "The treatment they're selling is a complete lie."

Olivia's face fell. "I kind of expected that."

"They're really doing it to erase our memories of what Di Mon is calling the Grianach Outbreak. As if it was a plague." Voltan watched as his sister's eyes widened in wonder. A moment later her brow creased and she frowned.

"How can they do that?"

"I don't know, but it doesn't matter. They can do it. What's important, though," he added quickly, hating himself for bringing extra stress to his sister, "is that I've figured out a way around it."

He explained what was contained in the vial, how it worked, and how there was only one dose.

"It's yours if you want it," he finished.

Olivia pulled herself up against the back of her bed as she cradled the vial in her hands. "You're a genius, you know that?"

Voltan's face flushed and he looked down. "Only because of what Prokhor engineered in us."

"You're a genius," she said firmly. Although her face had more lines than he remembered, her eyes retained some of their warmth, despite all the pain she'd gone through. Voltan's chest relaxed. She had looked after him — after all of them — for so long, and no matter what happened she still managed to find the strength to be there for him. He felt stupid and childish for running away into Prokhor's grasp simply because she had been overwhelmed, for a short while, by everyone else's needs.

"Thank you for offering this to me," she said finally, handing him the vial. "I am honored that you would think of me."

"Olivia, there's no one more deserving."

She shook her head. "I killed Pleo, Voltan. I don't want to remember that. I want to remember the good times we had together, and if that's what the Lorel is offering, via Di Mon's treatment, I'm going to take it." She turned to look out the window. The sun had risen higher and cast an oblique rectangle of the window into the room, which sent a diffuse glow over Voltan's hands.

"You didn't kill him, Olivia," he said softly, for what felt like the hundredth time. "But there are things you want to remember, aren't there?" He felt a lump form in his throat. "Your time with Faren? The refugees? Was none of it good?"

Olivia smiled, then frowned at the thought of Faren, an array of emotions rippling through her. "There were some good times," she murmured.

"Don't you want to remember those?"

"What about you, little brother?" She put her hand on his head.

He ducked to the side and grabbed her hand. "This isn't about me. Don't worry about me."

She smiled at him. "You've grown so much."

Voltan wanted to fix everything that had gone wrong, all at once, and felt a mixture of frustration and pain tighten in his chest. Taking a deep breath, he said, "I think you should take this vial, Olivia."

She shook her head, the sadness returning to her body as she sank into the bed. "I can't, Voltan." After a moment, she made a conscious effort to straighten. "But you're right. There were some things I don't want to forget. So how about this. I tell you those things now, and after I've forgotten, you can fill in the details to try and help me remember the good parts. It'll be like when people tell you about all the cute stuff you did when you were a baby."

Voltan took some time to absorb her suggestion. He, too, had been hoping to forget a lot of what had gone on, and to have the burden of being custodian of her good memories on him was a bit overwhelming. He looked at his sister, though, and thought of how much she had gone through, and how much she had done for him. Most of her life had been spent taking care of him and others. It was about time someone took care of her.

"All right," he said, "it's a plan. So tell me about Faren."

Olivia did.

Epilogue

Olivia's first question after she awoke from the treatment was, "Where's Pleo?"

Voltan put on a good show in front of the medics supervising the treatment, and to all appearances it seemed like the erasure had worked on him, as well.

Over time, he filled Olivia in on what had happened, leaving out the part about Pleo becoming the leader of the child warriors. "Olivia, what I am going to tell you will sound far-fetched or almost like a sick joke, but I swear to you with all of my heart that it's true. You can't tell anyone, though." Enough truths were there for the story to hold, and Olivia went through a second period of mourning over Pleo's death in the war. Eventually her pain subsided, things got back to normal in Grianach, and he and Olivia took over management of the spaceport where their parents had left off.

It had been a month since the treatments. The Ald'erda family had not escaped all blame for what became known as the Grianach Outbreak. However, Laedan Ald'erda was deemed to have paid by due process of Sword Law for his attempt to develop performance-enhancing drugs based on forbidden Lorel science. The nature of the drugs remained the source of gossip, but the official story was they were meant to be a cure-all for illnesses a highborn could overcome, as well as performance-enhancers for the skills a warrior needed on the challenge floor and in space. In other words, something any wise citizen should have suspected of being "snake oil" as well as contraband. What they'd really caused, according the official story, was psychotic side effects. Now the dead had been mopped up, the guilty excused, and the injured compensated— as long as guilty and innocent alike accepted treatment to prevent the risk of any further complications.

There were a few men and women who decried Di Mon as a corrupt liar, refused treatment, and told wild tales about what had really happened. They were usually gone the next day, and no one but Voltan seemed to pick up on it. Nestor was appointed Sheriff of Grianach for five years, which caused more stir on Fountain Court, for the sake of Nestor's Nersallian origins, than the Grianach Outbreak.

Voltan had taken to playing the eliox for reasons he couldn't explain. He practiced every night, the ringing chords becoming more and more harmonious with each hour he devoted to it. One evening, he'd finished playing and lay down to sleep, his fingers still humming with the music. He was just about to put the lights out when he saw her.

Dartha Lorel appeared shimmering above the eliox like a ghost. Voltan wished, not for the first time, that he were sharing a room with his brother Pleo again. He clutched at the bed sheets, pulling them up to his neckline as he fought the urge to tremble.

"You play well," she said.

Voltan sat with his gaze fixed on the eliox where it sat on a chair across the floor from him. "Are— are you the eliox?" he asked. His fingertips tingled from clutching his sheets too tightly.

"Oh, no," she said, becoming more and more transparent. "I am just a projection, child. And there's nothing here — now — that I can animate to give me substance." She smiled. "The eliox is simply made of something I've been stored in."

Voltan's mind flashed back to the nested web of Prokhor's deception, and the hairs on his arms bristled. He'd tried to transform some aspects of the experience into good, and dreaded the thought that the eliox, too, could be a further instrument of evil. "Did Prokhor know?" Voltan blurted out.

"No, not about the eliox particularly. But it was the one thing I was certain he would take everywhere. That, and the seka in his own bones and laboratory instruments. On the ship, of course, because it's Monatese, there were— but my

job is done and my coherence of consciousness is failing."
She tilted her head to one side in a thoughtful manner. "I
should probably not have manifest to you. But a persona
can become a little incoherent — space drunk, if you like —
before dissolution."

Coherence of consciousness was like grip. Voltan has
read about it in Prokhor's reference materials. "Are you...
dying?" he asked, struck with a pang he couldn't explain,
only that it felt akin to the loss of everything he'd done in
Prokhor's laboratory.

The fading projection gave him a perfectly ordinary smile.
"I'm what we call a sheut. A sort of subroutine or, what the
Reetions might call an AI persona. Sheuts don't die," she
said. "I'm Dartha Lorel, and while I won't remember my
experiences as Prokhor's minder, I'm still alive somewhere
else. In parallel. But may I say, child, it's been a privilege to
meet you. Maybe we'll meet in person someday."

Then she was gone. He lay back in bed, wondering, and
fell asleep to dream of proteins.

The next morning, Voltan descended the stairs for breakfast, and stared at Di Mon where he found him sitting
around the kitchen table, talking with Nestor and Remei.

"I would think a Liege of Fountain Court had better
things to do than shepherd a wayward Nersallian," Nestor
said playfully as he passed some spices to his wife. "Even if
the Nersallian is one of his sheriffs."

Di Mon allowed himself a smile, and said nothing.

"Clearly the Empire is getting dull. Maybe we need to
take up hobbies," Nestor went on.

"Oh, I assure you it is not dull on Gelion," Di Mon said,
dryly. "I just have a masochistic desire to be insulted by a
half-Demish Nersallian and his Nesak wife."

Remei put down her knife and wrapped her arms around
Nestor. "Well, whether it's dull on Fountain Court or not,
I'm just glad my husband's home to stay." She glowed
before turning to Di Mon again. "Besides, there's enough
work to be done here."

Di Mon nodded. "All your efforts are admirable, Remei.
But I must emphasize, again, that you owe Monitum
nothing."

Remei frowned and worked up an expression of annoyance. "Oh, pffft. It doesn't matter what we owe. The region needs hands to rebuild it and it doesn't matter where they come from. For once, Di Mon, I'm glad you asked Nestor to help."

Di Mon swallowed hard as Nestor shot him an amazed look. "If I didn't know better, I'd think Remei was starting to like you," said Nestor. "Did the universe spin on its head when we weren't watching?"

"Maybe," Di Mon said, much too thoughtfully, and looked away. A frown creased his forehead.

Remei brushed a glass off the counter as she turned with a cutting board, and it shattered loudly on the floor. She, Nestor, Enid and Olivia all flinched and stood still for several seconds as fleeting impressions of chaos — of refugees scattering and fleeing — rippled through their minds. The feelings could not be completely erased, and although Voltan was glad that enough memory had been left for everyone to be whole, it hurt him to see them touched by echoes of horrors they didn't fully understand. Nestor's first flight after the treatment had nearly killed him, as he had been overcome with inexplicable agony, and almost lost himself to gap. But he'd pulled out of it, and was flying as usual again.

The adults fell to talking about keeping the peace in Grianach and business at the spaceport, Di Mon looking as relaxed as Voltan could remember him being.

Voltan abandoned the kitchen for the living room where he found his sister.

Olivia was pregnant, and although she didn't yet show, she knew. She touched Voltan's arm lightly. "I felt something," she whispered. "And saw him again." She had been having vague clear-dreams where she described someone exactly like Faren, and Voltan felt relieved that the baby's father still retained some presence in her life. "Can you tell me more about him?" She traced a finger up and down her forearm unconsciously, occasionally resting her knuckles on her bicep.

Voltan petted Cam and took a deep breath. He spoke and tried to describe with as much detail as she had given him before, using some of her very words he had committed to memory. Wherever possible he avoided fabricating or interpreting, instead trying to serve as a focusing mirror through which she could regain some of her missing life.

When Olivia was satisfied, Voltan got up and grabbed the eliox from the corner.

The adults came in, and Di Mon remarked on the unusual instrument. "I've only ever seen one like it, before," he admitted. "In a museum on Sanctuary."

After some words of encouragement from his family, Voltan played a Monatese folksong, the rings echoing through the house as the wind drifted in through an open window. The music made it easier for him to breathe.

Made in the USA
Charleston, SC
07 November 2013